A COURT OF FROST AND STARLIGHT

BOOKS BY SARAH J. MAAS

The Throne of Glass series

The Assassin's Blade
Throne of Glass
Crown of Midnight
Heir of Fire
Queen of Shadows
Empire of Storms
Tower of Dawn

•

The Throne of Glass Coloring Book

A Court of Thorns and Roses series

A Court of Thorns and Roses
A Court of Mist and Fury
A Court of Wings and Ruin
A Court of Frost and Starlight

•

A Court of Thorns and Roses Coloring Book

A COURT OF FROST AND STARLIGHT

SARAH J. MAAS

BLOOMSBURY

NEW YORK LONDON OXFORD NEW DELHI SYDNEY

BLOOMSBURY YA
Bloomsbury Publishing Inc., part of Bloomsbury Publishing Plc
1385 Broadway, New York, NY 10018

BLOOMSBURY and the Diana logo are trademarks of Bloomsbury Publishing Plc

First published in the United States of America in May 2018 by Bloomsbury YA

Text copyright © 2018 by Sarah J. Maas
Map copyright © 2017 by Kelly de Groot
Exclusive and special edition endpapers copyright © by Monolime

Bloomsbury books may be purchased for business or promotional use. For information
on bulk purchases please contact Macmillan Corporate and Premium Sales Department at
specialmarkets@macmillan.com

Library of Congress Cataloging-in-Publication Data
Names: Maas, Sarah J., author
Title: A court of frost and starlight / by Sarah J. Maas.
Description: New York : Bloomsbury, 2018.
Summary: As Feyre navigates her first Winter Solstice as High Lady, she finds that those
dearest to her have more wounds than she anticipated—scars that will have a far-reaching
impact on the future of their court.
Identifiers: LCCN 2017056214
ISBN 978-1-68119-631-2 (hardcover) • ISBN 978-1-68119-906-1 (e-book)
Subjects: | CYAC: Fantasy. | Fairies—Fiction. | Winter solstice—Fiction.
Classification: LCC PZ7.M111575 Cj 2018 | DDC [Fic]—dc23
LC record available at https://lccn.loc.gov/2017056214

ISBN 978-1-5476-0035-9 (exclusive edition) • ISBN 978-1-5476-0038-0 (special edition)

Book design by Donna Mark
Typeset by Westchester Publishing Services
Printed and bound in the U.S.A. by Berryville Graphics Inc., Berryville, Virginia
2 4 6 8 10 9 7 5 3 1

All papers used by Bloomsbury Publishing Plc are natural, recyclable products
made from wood grown in well-managed forests. The manufacturing processes
conform to the environmental regulations of the country of origin.

To be kept up-to-date about our authors and books, please visit www.bloomsbury.com/newsletters
and sign up for our newsletters, including news about Sarah J. Maas.

To the readers who look up at the stars and wish

Prythian

Illyrian Mountains

Illyrian Steppes

The Prison

Velaris

Night Court

Court of Nightmares

Hybern

Day Court

Palace

Dawn Court

Weaver's Cottage

Under the Mountain

Winter Court

Adriata

Summer Court

Autumn Court

The Forest House

Spring Court

The Wall

Feyre's Village

Mortal Lands

Vallahan

Montesere

Rask

Faerie Realms

North to Faerie Realms

South to Mortal Lands

The Wall

Scythia

Mortal Lands

A COURT OF FROST AND STARLIGHT

CHAPTER
1

Feyre

The first snow of winter had begun whipping through Velaris an hour earlier.

The ground had finally frozen solid last week, and by the time I'd finished devouring my breakfast of toast and bacon, washed down with a heady cup of tea, the pale cobblestones were dusted with fine, white powder.

I had no idea where Rhys was. He hadn't been in bed when I'd awoken, the mattress on his side already cold. Nothing unusual, as we were both busy to the point of exhaustion these days.

Seated at the long cherrywood dining table at the town house, I frowned at the whirling snow beyond the leaded glass windows.

Once, I had dreaded that first snow, had lived in terror of long, brutal winters.

But it had been a long, brutal winter that had brought me so deep into the woods that day nearly two years ago. A long, brutal winter that had made me desperate enough to kill a wolf, that had eventually led me here—to this life, this . . . happiness.

The snow fell, thick clumps plopping onto the dried grass of the tiny front lawn, crusting the spikes and arches of the decorative fence beyond it.

Deep inside me, rising with every swirling flake, a sparkling, crisp power stirred. I was High Lady of the Night Court, yes, but also one blessed with the gifts of all the courts. It seemed Winter now wanted to play.

Finally awake enough to be coherent, I lowered the shield of black adamant guarding my mind and cast a thought down the soul-bridge between me and Rhys. *Where'd you fly off to so early?*

My question faded into blackness. A sure sign that Rhys was nowhere near Velaris. Likely not even within the borders of the Night Court. Also not unusual—he'd been visiting our war allies these months to solidify our relationships, build trade, and keep tabs on their post-wall intentions. When my own work allowed it, I often joined him.

I scooped up my plate, draining my tea to the dregs, and padded toward the kitchen. Playing with ice and snow could wait.

Nuala was already preparing for lunch at the worktable, no sign of her twin, Cerridwen, but I waved her off as she made to take my dishes. "I can wash them," I said by way of greeting.

Up to the elbows in making some sort of meat pie, the half-wraith gave me a grateful smile and let me do it. A female of few words, though neither twin could be considered shy. Certainly not when they worked—spied—for both Rhys and Azriel.

"It's still snowing," I observed rather pointlessly, peering out the kitchen window at the garden beyond as I rinsed off the plate, fork, and cup. Elain had already readied the garden for winter, veiling the more delicate bushes and beds with burlap. "I wonder if it'll let up at all."

Nuala laid the ornate lattice crust atop the pie and began pinching the edges together, her shadowy fingers making quick, deft work of it. "It'll be nice to have a white Solstice," she said, voice lilting and yet hushed. Full of whispers and shadows. "Some years, it can be fairly mild."

Right. The Winter Solstice. In a week. I was still new enough to being High Lady that I had no idea what my formal role was to be. If we'd have a High Priestess do some odious ceremony, as Ianthe had done the year before—

A year. Gods, nearly a year since Rhys had called in his bargain, desperate to get me away from the poison of the Spring Court, to save me from my despair. Had he been only a minute later, the Mother knew what would have happened. Where I'd now be.

Snow swirled and eddied in the garden, catching in the brown fibers of the burlap covering the shrubs.

My mate—who had worked so hard and so selflessly, all without hope that I would ever be with him.

We had both fought for that love, bled for it. Rhys had died for it.

I still saw that moment, in my sleeping and waking dreams. How his face had looked, how his chest had not risen, how the bond between us had shredded into ribbons. I still felt it, that hollowness in my chest where the bond had been, where *he* had been. Even now, with that bond again flowing between us like a river of star-flecked night, the echo of its vanishing lingered. Drew me from sleep; drew me from a conversation, a painting, a meal.

Rhys knew exactly why there were nights when I would cling tighter to him, why there were moments in the bright, clear sunshine that I would grip his hand. He knew, because *I* knew why his eyes sometimes turned distant, why he occasionally just blinked at all of us as if not quite believing it and rubbed his chest as if to ease an ache.

Working had helped. Both of us. Keeping busy, keeping focused—I sometimes dreaded the quiet, idle days when all those thoughts snared me at last. When there was nothing but me and my mind, and that memory of Rhys lying dead on the rocky ground, the King of Hybern snapping my father's neck, all those Illyrians blasted out of the sky and falling to earth as ashes.

Perhaps one day, even the work wouldn't be a battlement to keep the memories out.

Mercifully, plenty of work remained for the foreseeable future. Rebuilding Velaris after the attacks from Hybern being only one of many monumental tasks. For other tasks required doing as well—both in Velaris and beyond it: in the Illyrian Mountains, in the Hewn City, in the vastness of the entire Night Court. And then there were the other courts of Prythian. And the new, emerging world beyond.

But for now: Solstice. The longest night of the year. I turned from the window to Nuala, who was still fussing over the edges of her pie. "It's a special holiday here as well, right?" I asked casually. "Not just in Winter and Day." And Spring.

"Oh, yes," Nuala said, stooping over the worktable to examine her pie. Skilled spy—trained by Azriel himself—and master cook. "We love it dearly. It's intimate, warm, lovely. Presents and music and food, sometimes feasting under the starlight . . ." The opposite of the enormous, wild, days-long party I'd been subjected to last year. But—presents.

I had to buy presents for all of them. Not had to, but *wanted* to.

Because all my friends, now my family, had fought and bled and nearly died as well.

I shut out the image that tore through my mind: Nesta, leaning over a wounded Cassian, the two of them prepared to die together against the King of Hybern. My father's corpse behind them.

I rolled my neck. We could use something to celebrate. It had become so rare for all of us to be gathered for more than an hour or two.

Nuala went on, "It's a time of rest, too. And a time to reflect on the darkness—how it lets the light shine."

"Is there a ceremony?"

The half-wraith shrugged. "Yes, but none of us go. It's more for those who wish to honor the light's rebirth, usually by spending the entire night sitting in absolute darkness." A ghost of a smirk. "It's not quite such a novelty for my sister and me. Or for the High Lord."

I tried not to look too relieved that I wouldn't be dragged to a temple for hours as I nodded.

Setting my clean dishes to dry on the little wooden rack beside the sink, I wished Nuala luck on lunch, and headed upstairs to dress. Cerridwen had already laid out clothes, but there was still no sign of Nuala's twin as I donned the heavy charcoal sweater, the tight black leggings, and fleece-lined boots before loosely braiding back my hair.

A year ago, I'd been stuffed into fine gowns and jewels, made to parade in front of a preening court who'd gawked at me like a prized breeding mare.

Here . . . I smiled at the silver-and-sapphire band on my left hand. The ring I'd won for myself from the Weaver in the Wood.

My smile faded a bit.

I could see her, too. See Stryga standing before the King of

Hybern, covered in the blood of her prey, as he took her head in his hands and snapped her neck. Then threw her to his beasts.

I clenched my fingers into a fist, breathing in through my nose, out through my mouth, until the lightness in my limbs faded, until the walls of the room stopped pressing on me.

Until I could survey the blend of personal objects in Rhys's room—our room. It was by no means a small bedroom, but it had lately started to feel . . . tight. The rosewood desk against one wall was covered in papers and books from both of our own dealings; my jewelry and clothes now had to be divided between here and my old bedroom. And then there were the weapons.

Daggers and blades, quivers and bows. I scratched my head at the heavy, wicked-looking *mace* that Rhys had somehow dumped beside the desk without my noticing.

I didn't even want to know. Though I had no doubt Cassian was somehow behind it.

We could, of course, store everything in the pocket between realms, but . . . I frowned at my own set of Illyrian blades, leaning against the towering armoire.

If we got snowed in, perhaps I'd use the day to organize things. Find room for everything. Especially that mace.

It would be a challenge, since Elain still occupied a bedroom down the hall. Nesta had chosen her own home across the city, one that I opted to not think about for too long. Lucien, at least, had taken up residence in an elegant apartment down by the river the day after he'd returned from the battlefields. And the Spring Court.

I hadn't asked Lucien any questions about that visit—to Tamlin.

Lucien hadn't explained the black eye and cut lip, either. He'd only asked Rhys and me if we knew of a place to stay in Velaris, since he did not wish to inconvenience us further by staying at the town house, and did not wish to be isolated at the House of Wind.

He hadn't mentioned Elain, or his proximity to her. Elain had not asked him to stay, or to go. And whether she cared about the bruises on his face, she certainly hadn't let on.

But Lucien had remained, and found ways to keep busy, often gone for days or weeks at a time.

Yet even with Lucien and Nesta staying in their own apartments, the town house was a bit small these days. Even more so if Mor, Cassian, and Azriel stayed over. And the House of Wind was too big, too formal, too far from the city proper. Nice for a night or two, but . . . I loved this house.

It was my home. The first I'd really had in the ways that counted.

And it'd be nice to celebrate the Solstice here. With all of them, crowded as it might be.

I scowled at the pile of papers I had to sort through: letters from other courts, priestesses angling for positions, and kingdoms both human and faerie. I'd put them off for weeks now, and had finally set aside this morning to wade through them.

High Lady of the Night Court, Defender of the Rainbow and the . . . Desk.

I snorted, flicking my braid over a shoulder. Perhaps my Solstice gift to myself would be to hire a personal secretary. Someone to read and answer those things, to sort out what was vital and what could be put aside. Because a little extra time to myself, for *Rhys* . . .

I'd look through the court budget that Rhys never really cared to follow and see what could be moved around for the possibility of such a thing. For him and for me.

I knew our coffers ran deep, knew we could easily afford it and not make so much as a dent in our fortune, but I didn't mind the work. I loved the work, actually. This territory, its people—they were as much my heart as my mate. Until yesterday, nearly every waking hour had been packed with helping them. Until I'd been politely, graciously, told to *go home and enjoy the holiday.*

In the wake of the war, the people of Velaris had risen to the challenge of rebuilding and helping their own. Before I'd even come up with an idea of *how* to help them, multiple societies had been created to assist the city. So I'd volunteered with a handful of them for tasks ranging from finding homes for those displaced by the destruction to visiting families affected during the war to helping those without shelter or belongings ready for winter with new coats and supplies.

All of it was vital; all of it was good, satisfying work. And yet . . . there was more. There was *more* that I could do to help. Personally. I just hadn't figured it out yet.

It seemed I wasn't the only one eager to assist those who'd lost so much. With the holiday, a surge of fresh volunteers had arrived, cramming the public hall near the Palace of Thread and Jewels, where so many of the societies were headquartered. *Your help has been crucial, Lady,* one charity matron had said to me yesterday. *You have been here nearly every day—you have worked yourself to the bone. Take the week off. You've earned it. Celebrate with your mate.*

I'd tried to object, insisting that there were still more coats to hand out, more firewood to be distributed, but the faerie had just motioned to the crowded public hall around us, filled to the brim with volunteers. *We have more help than we know what to do with.*

When I'd tried objecting again, she'd shooed me out the front door. And shut it behind me.

Point taken. The story had been the same at every other organization I'd stopped by yesterday afternoon. *Go home and enjoy the holiday.*

So I had. At least, the first part. The *enjoying* bit, however . . .

Rhys's answer to my earlier inquiry about his whereabouts finally flickered down the bond, carried on a rumble of dark, glittering power. *I'm at Devlon's camp.*

It took you this long to respond? It was a long distance to the Illyrian Mountains, yes, but it shouldn't have taken minutes to hear back.

A sensual huff of laughter. *Cassian was ranting. He didn't take a breath.*

My poor Illyrian baby. We certainly do torment you, don't we?

Rhys's amusement rippled toward me, caressing my innermost self with night-veiled hands. But it halted, vanishing as quickly as it had come. *Cassian's getting into it with Devlon. I'll check in later.* With a loving brush against my senses, he was gone.

I'd get a full report about it soon, but for now . . .

I smiled at the snow waltzing outside the windows.

CHAPTER
2

Rhysand

It was barely nine in the morning, and Cassian was already pissed.

The watery winter sun tried and failed to bleed through the clouds looming over the Illyrian Mountains, the wind a boom across the gray peaks. Snow already lay inches deep over the bustling camp, a vision of what would soon befall Velaris.

It had been snowing when I departed at dawn—perhaps there would be a good coating already on the ground by the time I returned. I hadn't had a chance to ask Feyre about it during our brief conversation down the bond minutes ago, but perhaps she would go for a walk with me through it. Let me show her how the City of Starlight glistened under fresh snow.

Indeed, my mate and city seemed a world away from the hive of activity in the Windhaven camp, nestled in a wide, high mountain pass. Even the bracing wind that swept between the peaks, belying the camp's very name by whipping up dervishes of snow, didn't deter the Illyrians from going about their daily chores.

For the warriors: training in the various rings that opened onto a sheer drop to the small valley floor below, those not present out on patrol. For the males who hadn't made the cut: tending to various trades, whether merchants or blacksmiths or cobblers. And for the females: drudgery.

They didn't see it as such. None of them did. But their required tasks, whether old or young, remained the same: cooking, cleaning, child-rearing, clothes-making, laundry . . . There was honor in such tasks—pride and good work to be found in them. But not when every single one of the females here was *expected* to do it. And if they shirked those duties, either one of the half-dozen camp-mothers or whatever males controlled their lives would punish them.

So it had been, as long as I'd known this place, for my mother's people. The world had been reborn during the war months before, the wall blasted to nothingness, and yet some things did not alter. Especially here, where change was slower than the melting glaciers scattered amongst these mountains. Traditions going back thousands of years, left mostly unchallenged.

Until us. Until now.

Drawing my attention away from the bustling camp beyond the edge of the chalk-lined training rings where we stood, I schooled my face into neutrality as Cassian squared off against Devlon.

"The girls are busy with preparations for the Solstice," the camp-lord was saying, his arms crossed over his barrel chest. "The wives need all the help they can get, if all's to be ready in time. They can practice next week."

I'd lost count of how many variations of this conversation we'd had during the decades Cassian had been pushing Devlon on this.

The wind whipped Cassian's dark hair, but his face remained hard as granite as he said to the warrior who had begrudgingly trained us, "The girls can help their mothers *after* training is done

11

for the day. We'll cut practice down to two hours. The rest of the day will be enough to assist in the preparations."

Devlon slid his hazel eyes to where I lingered a few feet away. "Is it an order?"

I held that gaze. And despite my crown, my power, I tried not to fall back into the trembling child I'd been five centuries ago, that first day Devlon had towered over me and then hurled me into the sparring ring. "If Cassian says it's an order, then it is."

It had occurred to me, during the years we'd been waging this same battle with Devlon and the Illyrians, that I could simply rip into his mind, all their minds, and make them agree. Yet there were some lines I could not, would not cross. And Cassian would never forgive me.

Devlon grunted, his breath a curl of steam. "An hour."

"Two hours," Cassian countered, wings flaring slightly as he held a hard line that I'd been called in this morning to help him maintain.

It had to be bad, then, if my brother had asked me to come. Really damn bad. Perhaps we needed a permanent presence out here, until the Illyrians remembered things like consequences.

But the war had impacted us all, and with the rebuilding, with the human territories crawling out to meet us, with other Fae kingdoms looking toward a wall-less world and wondering what shit they could get away with . . . We didn't have the resources to station someone out here. Not yet. Perhaps next summer, if the climate elsewhere was calm enough.

Devlon's cronies loitered in the nearest sparring ring, sizing up Cassian and me, the same way they had our entire lives. We'd slaughtered enough of them in the Blood Rite all those centuries ago that they still kept back, but . . . It had been the Illyrians who had bled and fought this summer. Who had suffered the most losses as they took on the brunt of Hybern and the Cauldron.

That any of the warriors survived was a testament to their skill and Cassian's leadership, but with the Illyrians isolated and idle up here, that loss was starting to shape itself into something ugly. Dangerous.

None of us had forgotten that during Amarantha's reign, a few of the war-bands had gleefully bowed to her. And I knew none of the Illyrians had forgotten that we'd spent those first few months after her downfall hunting down those rogue groups. And ending them.

Yes, a presence here was needed. But later.

Devlon pushed, crossing his muscled arms. "The boys need a nice Solstice after all they endured. Let the girls give one to them."

The bastard certainly knew what weapons to wield, both physical and verbal.

"Two hours in the ring each morning," Cassian said with that same hard tone that even I knew not to push unless I wanted a flat-out brawl. He didn't break Devlon's gaze. "The *boys* can help decorate, clean, and cook. They've got two hands."

"Some do," Devlon said. "Some came home without one."

I felt, more than saw, the wound strike deep in Cassian.

It was the cost of leading my armies: each injury, death, scar— he took them all as his own personal failings. And being around these warriors, seeing those missing limbs and brutal injuries still healing or that would never heal . . .

"They practice for ninety minutes," I said, soothing the dark power that began to roil in my veins, seeking a path into the

13

world, and slid my chilled hands into my pockets. Cassian, wisely, pretended to look outraged, his wings spreading wide. Devlon opened his mouth, but I cut him off before he could shout something truly stupid. "An hour and a half every morning, then they do the housework, the males pitching in whenever they can." I glanced toward the permanent tents and small stone and wood houses scattered along the wide pass and up into the tree-crusted peaks behind us. "Do not forget that a great number of the females, Devlon, also suffered losses. Perhaps not a hand, but their husbands and sons and brothers were out on those battlefields. Everyone helps prepare for the holiday, and everyone gets to train."

I jerked my chin at Cassian, indicating for him to follow me to the house across the camp that we now kept as our semi-permanent base of operations. There wasn't a surface inside where I hadn't taken Feyre—the kitchen table being my particular favorite, thanks to those raw initial days after we'd first mated, when I could barely stand to be near her and not be buried inside her.

How long ago, how distant, those days seemed. Another lifetime ago.

I needed a holiday.

Snow and ice crunched under our boots as we aimed for the narrow, two-level stone house by the tree line.

Not a holiday to rest, not to visit anywhere, but just to spend more than a handful of hours in the same bed as my mate.

To get more than a few hours to sleep *and* bury myself in her. It seemed to be one or the other these days. Which was utterly unacceptable. And had turned me about twenty kinds of foolish.

Last week had been so stupidly busy and I'd been so desperate for the feel and taste of her that I'd taken her during the flight down from the House of Wind to the town house. High above Velaris—for all to see, if it weren't for the cloaking I had thrown into place. It'd required some careful maneuvering, and I'd planned for months now on actually making a moment of it, but with her against me like that, alone in the skies, all it had taken was one look into those blue-gray eyes and I was unfastening her pants.

A moment later, I'd been inside her, and had nearly sent us crashing into the rooftops like an Illyrian whelp. Feyre had just laughed.

I'd climaxed at the husky sound of it.

It had not been my finest moment, and I had no doubt I'd sink to lower levels before the Winter Solstice bought us a day's reprieve.

I choked my rising desire until it was nothing but a vague roaring in the back of my mind, and didn't speak until Cassian and I were nearly through the wooden front door.

"Anything else I should know about while I'm here?" I knocked the snow from my boots against the door frame and stepped into the house. That kitchen table lay smack in the middle of the front room. I banished the image of Feyre bent over it.

Cassian blew out a breath and shut the door behind him before tucking in his wings and leaning against it. "Dissension's brewing. With so many clans gathering for the Solstice, it'll be a chance for them to spread it even more."

A flicker of my power had a fire roaring in the hearth, the small downstairs warming swiftly. It was barely a whisper of magic, yet its release eased that near-constant strain of keeping all that I was, all that dark power, in check. I took up a spot against that damned table and crossed my arms. "We've dealt with this shit before. We'll deal with it again."

Cassian shook his head, the shoulder-length dark hair shining in the watery light leaking through the front windows. "It's not like it was before. Before, you, me, and Az—we were resented for what we are, who we are. But this time . . . *we* sent them to battle. *I* sent them, Rhys. And now it's not only the warrior-pricks who are grumbling, but also the females. They believe you and I marched them south as revenge for our own treatment as children; they think we specifically stationed some of the males on the front lines as payback."

Not good. Not good at all. "We have to handle this carefully, then. Find out where this poison comes from and put an end to it— peacefully," I clarified when he lifted his brows. "We can't kill our way out of this one."

Cassian scratched at his jaw. "No, we can't." It wouldn't be like hunting down those rogue war-bands who'd terrorized any in their path. Not at all.

He surveyed the dim house, the fire crackling in the hearth, where we'd seen my mother cook so many meals during our training. An old, familiar ache filled my chest. This entire house, every inch of it, was full of the past. "A lot of them are coming in for the Solstice," he went on. "I can stay here, keep an eye on things. Maybe hand out presents to the children, some of the wives. Things that they really need but are too proud to ask for."

It was a solid idea. But—"It can wait. I want you home for Solstice."

"I don't mind—"

"I want you home. In Velaris," I added when he opened his mouth to spew some Illyrian loyalist bullshit that he still believed, even after they had treated him like less than nothing his entire life. "We're spending Solstice together. All of us."

Even if I had to give them a direct order as High Lord to do it. Cassian angled his head. "What's eating at you?"

"Nothing."

As far as things went, I had little to complain about. Taking my mate to bed on a regular basis wasn't exactly a pressing issue. Or anyone's concern but our own.

"Wound a little tight, Rhys?"

Of course he'd seen right through it.

I sighed, frowning at the ancient, soot-speckled ceiling. We'd celebrated the Solstice in this house, too. My mother always had gifts for Azriel and Cassian. For the latter, the initial Solstice we'd shared here had been the first time he'd received *any* sort of gift, Solstice or not. I could still see the tears Cassian had tried to hide as he'd opened his presents, and the tears in my mother's eyes as she watched him. "I want to jump ahead to next week."

"Sure that power of yours can't do it for you?"

I leveled a dry look at him. Cassian just gave me a cocky grin back.

I never stopped being grateful for them—my friends, my family, who looked at that power of mine and did not balk, did not become scented with fear. Yes, I could scare the shit out of them sometimes, but we *all* did that to each other. Cassian had terrified me more times than I wanted to admit, one of them being mere months ago.

Twice. Twice, in the span of a matter of weeks, it had happened.

I still saw him being hauled by Azriel off that battlefield, blood spilling down his legs, into the mud, his wound a gaping maw that sliced down the center of his body.

And I still saw him as Feyre had seen him—after she'd let me into her mind to reveal what, exactly, had occurred between her sisters and the King of Hybern. Still saw Cassian, broken and bleeding on the ground, begging Nesta to run.

Cassian had not yet spoken of it. About what had occurred in those moments. About Nesta.

Cassian and my mate's sister did not speak to each other at all.

Nesta had successfully cloistered herself in some slummy apartment across the Sidra, refusing to interact with any of us save for a few brief visits with Feyre every month.

I'd have to find a way to fix that, too.

I saw how it ate away at Feyre. I still soothed her after she awoke, frantic, from nightmares about that day in Hybern when her sisters had been Made against their will. Nightmares about the moment when Cassian was near death and Nesta was sprawled over him, shielding him from that killing blow, and Elain—*Elain*—had taken up Azriel's dagger and killed the King of Hybern instead.

I rubbed my brows between my thumb and forefinger. "It's rough now. We're all busy, all trying to hold everything together." Az, Cassian, and I had yet again postponed our annual five days of hunting up at the cabin this fall. Put off for next year—again. "Come home for Solstice, and we can sit down and figure out a plan for the spring."

"Sounds like a festive event."

With my Court of Dreams, it always was.

But I made myself ask, "Is Devlon one of the would-be rebels?"

I prayed it wasn't true. I resented the male and his backwardness, but he'd been fair with Cassian, Azriel, and me under his watch. Treated us to the same rights as full-blooded Illyrian warriors. Still did that for all the bastard-born under his command. It was his absurd ideas about females that made me want to throttle him. Mist him. But if he had to be replaced, the Mother knew who would take his position.

Cassian shook his head. "I don't think so. Devlon shuts down any talk like that. But it only makes them more secretive, which makes it harder to find out who's spreading this bullshit around."

I nodded, standing. I had a meeting in Cesere with the two priestesses who had survived Hybern's massacre a year ago regarding how to handle pilgrims who wanted to come from outside our territory. Being late wouldn't lend any favors to my arguments to delay such a thing until the spring. "Keep an eye on it for the next few days, then come home. I want you there two nights before Solstice. And for the day after."

A hint of a wicked grin. "I assume our Solstice-day tradition will still be on, then. Despite you now being such a grown-up, mated male."

I winked at him. "I'd hate for you Illyrian babies to miss me."

Cassian chuckled. There were indeed some Solstice traditions that never grew tiresome, even after the centuries. I was almost at the door when Cassian said, "Is . . ." He swallowed.

I spared him the discomfort of trying to mask his interest. "Both sisters will be at the house. Whether they want to or not."

"Nesta will make things unpleasant if she decides she doesn't want to be there."

"She'll be there," I said, grinding my teeth, "and she'll be pleasant. She owes Feyre that much."

Cassian's eyes flickered. "How is she?"

I didn't bother to put any sort of spin on it. "Nesta is Nesta. She does what she wants, even if it kills her sister. I've offered her job after job, and she refuses them all." I sucked on my teeth. "Perhaps you can talk some sense into her over Solstice."

Cassian's Siphons gleamed atop his hands. "It'd likely end in violence."

It indeed would. "Then don't say a word to her. I don't care—just keep Feyre out of it. It's her day, too."

Because this Solstice . . . it was her birthday. Twenty-one years old.

It hit me for a moment, how small that number was.

My beautiful, strong, fierce mate, shackled to me—

"I know what that look means, you bastard," Cassian said roughly, "and it's bullshit. She loves you—in a way I've never seen anybody love anyone."

"It's hard sometimes," I admitted, staring toward the snow-coated field outside the house, the training rings and dwellings beyond it, "to remember that she picked it. Picked me. That it's not like my parents, shoved together."

Cassian's face turned uncharacteristically solemn, and he remained quiet for a moment before he said, "I get jealous sometimes. I'd never begrudge you for your happiness, but what you two have, Rhys . . ." He dragged a hand through his hair, his crimson Siphon glinting in the light streaming through the window. "It's the legends, the lies, they spin us when we're children. About the glory and wonder of the mating bond. I thought it was all bullshit. Then you two came along."

"She's turning twenty-one. *Twenty-one*, Cassian."

"So? Your mother was eighteen to your father's nine hundred."

"And she was miserable."

"Feyre is not your mother. And you are not your father." He looked me over. "Where is this coming from, anyway? Are things . . . not good?"

The opposite, actually. "I get this feeling," I said, pacing a step, the ancient wood floorboards creaking beneath my boots, my power a writhing, living thing prowling through my veins, "that it's all some sort of joke. Some sort of cosmic trick, and that no one—*no one*—can be this happy and not pay for it."

"You've already paid for it, Rhys. Both of you. And then some."

I waved a hand. "I just . . ." I trailed off, unable to finish the words.

Cassian stared at me for a long moment.

Then he crossed the distance between us, gathering me in an embrace so tight I could barely breathe. "You made it. *We* made it. You both endured enough that no one would blame you if you danced off into the sunset like Miryam and Drakon and never bothered with anything else again. But you are bothering—you're both still working to make this peace last. *Peace*, Rhys. We have *peace*, and the true kind. Enjoy it—enjoy each other. You paid the debt before it was ever a debt."

My throat tightened, and I gripped him hard around his wings, the scales of his leathers digging into my fingers. "What about you?" I asked, pulling away after a moment. "Are you . . . happy?"

Shadows darkened his hazel eyes. "I'm getting there."

A halfhearted answer.

I'd have to work on that, too. Perhaps there were threads to be pulled, woven together.

Cassian jerked his chin toward the door. "Get going, you bastard. I'll see you in three days."

I nodded, opening the door at last. But paused on the threshold. "Thanks, brother."

Cassian's crooked grin was bright, even if those shadows still guttered in his eyes. "It's an honor, my lord."

CHAPTER 3

Cassian

Cassian wasn't entirely certain that he could deal with Devlon and his warriors without throttling them. At least, not for the next good hour or so.

And since that would do little to help quell the murmurings of discontent, Cassian waited until Rhys had winnowed out into the snow and wind before vanishing himself.

Not winnowing, though that would have been one hell of a weapon against enemies in battle. He'd seen Rhys do it with devastating results. Az, too—in the strange way that Az could move through the world *without* technically winnowing.

He'd never asked. Azriel certainly had never explained.

But Cassian didn't mind his own method of moving: flying. It certainly had served him well enough in battle.

Stepping out the front door of the ancient wooden house so that Devlon and the other pricks in the sparring rings would see him, Cassian made a good show of stretching. First his arms, honed and still aching to pummel in a few Illyrian faces. Then his wings, wider and broader than theirs. They'd always resented that, perhaps more than anything else. He flared them until the strain along the powerful muscles and sinews was a pleasurable burn, his wings casting long shadows across the snow.

And with a mighty flap, he shot into the gray skies.

The wind was a roar around him, the temperature cold enough that his eyes watered. Bracing—freeing. He flapped higher, then banked left, aiming for the peaks behind the camp pass. No need to do a warning sweep over Devlon and the sparring rings.

Ignoring them, projecting the message that they weren't important enough to even be considered threats were far better ways of pissing them off. Rhys had taught him that. Long ago.

Catching an updraft that sent him soaring over the nearest peaks and then into the endless, snow-coated labyrinth of mountains that made up their homeland, Cassian breathed in deep. His flying leathers and gloves kept him warm enough, but his wings, exposed to the chill wind . . . The cold was sharp as a knife.

He could shield himself with his Siphons, had done it in the past. But today, this morning, he wanted that biting cold.

Especially with what he was about to do. Where he was going.

He would have known the path blindfolded, simply by listening to the wind through the mountains, inhaling the smell of the pine-crusted peaks below, the barren rock fields.

It was rare for him to make the trek. He usually only did it when his temper was likely to get the better of him, and he had enough lingering control to know he needed to head out for a few hours. Today was no exception.

In the distance, small, dark shapes shot through the sky. Warriors on patrol. Or perhaps armed escorts leading families to their Solstice reunions.

Most High Fae believed the Illyrians were the greatest menace in these mountains.

They didn't realize that far worse things prowled between the peaks. Some of them hunting on the winds, some crawling out from deep caverns in the rock itself.

Feyre had braved facing some of those things in the pine forests of the Steppes. To save Rhys. Cassian wondered if his brother had ever told her what dwelled in these mountains. Most had been slain by the Illyrians, or sent fleeing to those Steppes. But the most cunning of them, the most ancient . . . they had found ways to hide. To emerge on moonless nights to feed.

Even five centuries of training couldn't stop the chill that skittered down his spine as Cassian surveyed the empty, quiet mountains below and wondered what slept beneath the snow.

He cut northward, casting the thought from his mind. On the horizon, a familiar shape took form, growing larger with each flap of his wings.

Ramiel. The sacred mountain.

The heart of not only Illyria, but the entirety of the Night Court.

None were permitted on its barren, rocky slopes—save for the Illyrians, and only once a year at that. During the Blood Rite.

Cassian soared toward it, unable to resist Ramiel's ancient summons. Different—the mountain was so different from the barren, terrible presence of the lone peak in the center of Prythian. Ramiel had always felt alive, somehow. Awake and watchful.

He'd only set foot on it once, on that final day of the Rite. When he and his brothers, bloodied and battered, had scaled its side to reach the onyx monolith at its summit. He could still feel the crumbling rock beneath his boots, hear the rasp of his breathing as he half hauled Rhys up the slopes, Azriel providing cover behind. As one, the three of them had touched the stone—the first to reach its peak at the end of that brutal week. The uncontested winners.

The Rite hadn't changed in the centuries since. Early each spring, it still went on, hundreds of warrior-novices deposited across the mountains and forests surrounding the peak, the territory off-limits during the rest of the year to prevent any of the novices from scouting ahead for the best routes and traps to lay. There were varying qualifiers throughout the year to prove a novice's readiness, each slightly different depending on the camp. But the rules remained the same.

All novices competed with wings bound, no Siphons—a spell restraining all magic—and no supplies beyond the clothes on your back. The goal: make it to the summit of that mountain by the end of that week and touch the stone. The obstacles: the distance, the natural traps, and each other. Old feuds played out; new ones were born. Scores were settled.

A week of pointless bloodshed, Az insisted.

Rhys often agreed, though he often *also* agreed with Cassian's point: the Blood Rite offered an escape valve for dangerous tensions within the Illyrian community. Better to settle it during the Rite than risk civil war.

Illyrians were strong, proud, fearless. But peacemakers, they were not.

Perhaps he'd get lucky. Perhaps the Rite this spring would ease some of the malcontent. Hell, he'd offer to participate *himself*, if it meant quieting the grumbling.

They'd barely survived this war. They didn't need another one. Not with so many unknowns gathering outside their borders.

Ramiel rose higher still, a shard of stone piercing the gray sky. Beautiful and lonely. Eternal and ageless.

No wonder that first ruler of the Night Court had made this his insignia. Along with the three stars that only appeared for a brief window each year, framing the uppermost peak of Ramiel like a crown. It was during that window when the Rite occurred. Which had come first: the insignia or the Rite, Cassian didn't know. Had never really cared to find out.

The conifer forests and ravines that dotted the landscape flowing to Ramiel's foot gleamed under fresh snow. Empty and clean. No sign of the bloodshed that would occur come the start of spring.

The mountain neared, mighty and endless, so wide that he might as well have been a mayfly in the wind. Cassian soared toward Ramiel's southern face, rising high enough to catch a glimpse of the shining black stone jutting from its top.

Who had put that stone atop the peak, he didn't know, either. Legend said it had existed before the Night Court formed, before the Illyrians migrated from the Myrmidons, before humans had even walked the earth. Even with the fresh snow crusting Ramiel, none had touched the pillar of stone.

A thrill, icy and yet not unwelcome, flooded his veins.

It was rare for anyone in the Blood Rite to make it to the monolith. Since he and his brothers had done it five centuries ago, Cassian could recall only a dozen or so who'd not only reached the mountain, but also survived the climb. After a week of fighting, of running, of having to find and make your own weapons and food, that climb was worse than every horror before it. It was the true test of will, of courage. To climb when you had nothing left; to climb when your body begged you to stop . . . It was when the breaking usually occurred.

But when he'd touched the onyx monolith, when he'd felt that ancient force sing into his blood in the heartbeat before it had whisked him back to the safety of Devlon's camp . . . It had been worth it. To feel that.

With a solemn bow of his head toward Ramiel and the living stone atop it, Cassian caught another swift wind and soared southward.

An hour's flight had him approaching yet another familiar peak.

One that no one but him and his brothers bothered to come to. What he'd so badly needed to see, to feel, today.

Once, it had been as busy a camp as Devlon's.

Once. Before a bastard had been born in a freezing, lone tent on the outskirts of the village. Before they'd thrown a young, unwed mother out into the snow only days after giving birth, her babe in her arms. And then taken that babe mere years later, tossing him into the mud at Devlon's camp.

Cassian landed on the flat stretch of mountain pass, the snow-drifts higher than at Windhaven. Hiding any trace of the village that had stood here.

Only cinders and debris remained anyway.

He'd made sure of it.

When those who had been responsible for her suffering and tor-ment had been dealt with, no one had wanted to remain here a moment longer. Not with the shattered bone and blood coating every surface, staining every field and training ring. So they'd migrated, some blending into other camps, others making their own lives elsewhere. None had ever come back.

Centuries later, he didn't regret it.

Standing in the snow and wind, surveying the emptiness where he'd been born, Cassian didn't regret it for a heartbeat.

His mother had suffered every moment of her too-short life. It only grew worse after she'd given birth to him. Especially in the years after he'd been taken away.

And when he'd been strong and old enough to come back to look for her, she was gone.

They'd refused to tell him where she was buried. If they'd given her that honor, or if they'd thrown her body into an icy chasm to rot.

He still didn't know. Even with their final, rasping breaths, those who'd made sure she never knew happiness had refused to tell him. Had spat in his face and told him every awful thing they'd done to her.

He'd wanted to bury her in Velaris. Somewhere full of light and warmth, full of kind people. Far away from these mountains.

Cassian scanned the snow-covered pass. His memories here were murky: mud and cold and too-small fires. But he could recall a lilting, soft voice, and gentle, slender hands.

It was all he had of her.

Cassian dragged his hands through his hair, fingers catching on the wind-tangled snarls.

He knew why he'd come here, why he always came here. For all that Amren taunted him about being an Illyrian brute, he knew his own mind, his own heart.

Devlon was a fairer camp-lord than most. But for the females who were less fortunate, who were preyed upon or cast out, there was little mercy.

So training these women, giving them the resources and confidence to fight back, to look beyond their campfires . . . it was for her. For the mother buried here, perhaps buried nowhere. So it might never happen again. So his people, whom he still loved despite their faults, might one day become something *more*. Something better.

The unmarked, unknown grave in this pass was his reminder.

Cassian stood in silence for long minutes before turning his gaze westward. As if he might see all the way to Velaris.

Rhys wanted him home for the Solstice, and he'd obey.

Even if Nesta—

Nesta.

Even in his thoughts, her name clanged through him, hollow and cold.

Now wasn't the time to think of her. Not here.

He very rarely allowed himself to think of her, anyway. It usually didn't end well for whoever was in the sparring ring with him.

Spreading his wings wide, Cassian took a final glance around the camp he'd razed to the ground. Another reminder, too: of what he was capable of when pushed too far.

To be careful, even when Devlon and the others made him want to bellow. He and Az were the most powerful Illyrians in their long, bloody history. They wore an unprecedented seven Siphons each, just to handle the tidal wave of brute killing power they possessed. It was a gift and a burden that he'd never taken lightly.

Three days. He had three days until he was to go to Velaris.

He'd try to make them count.

CHAPTER
4

Feyre

The Rainbow was a hum of activity, even with the drifting veils of snow.

High Fae and faeries alike poured in and out of the various shops and studios, some perched on ladders to string up drooping garlands of pine and holly between the lampposts, some sweeping gathered clusters of snow from their doorsteps, some—no doubt artists— merely standing on the pale cobblestones and turning in place, faces uplifted to the gray sky, hair and skin and clothes dusted with fine powder.

Dodging one such person in the middle of the street—a faerie with skin like glittering onyx and eyes like swirling clusters of stars—I aimed for the front of a small, pretty gallery, its glass window revealing an assortment of paintings and pottery. The perfect place to do some Solstice shopping. A wreath of evergreen hung on the freshly painted blue door, brass bells dangling from its center.

The door: new. The display window: new.

Both had been shattered and stained with blood months ago. This entire street had.

It was an effort not to glance at the white-dusted stones of the street, sloping steeply down to the meandering Sidra at its base. To the walkway along the river, full of patrons and artists, where I had stood months ago and summoned wolves from those slumbering waters. Blood had been streaming down these cobblestones then, and there hadn't been singing and laughter in the streets, but screaming and pleading.

I took a sharp inhale through my nose, the chilled air tickling my nostrils. Slowly, I released it in a long breath, watching it cloud in front of me. Watching myself in the reflection of the store window: barely recognizable in my heavy gray coat, a red-and-gray scarf that I'd pilfered from Mor's closet, my eyes wide and distant.

I realized a heartbeat later that I was not the only one staring at myself.

Inside the gallery, no fewer than five people were doing their best not to gawk at me as they browsed the collection of paintings and pottery.

My cheeks warmed, heart a staccato beat, and I offered a tight smile before continuing on.

No matter that I'd spotted a piece that caught my eye. No matter that I *wanted* to go in.

I kept my gloved hands bundled in the pockets of my coat as I strode down the steep street, mindful of my steps on the slick cobblestones. While Velaris had plenty of spells upon it to keep the palaces and cafés and squares warm during the winter, it seemed that for this first snow, many of them had been lifted, as if everyone wanted to feel its chill kiss.

I'd indeed braved the walk from the town house, wanting to not only breathe in the crisp, snowy air, but to also just absorb the crackling excitement of those readying for Solstice, rather than merely winnowing or flying over them.

Though Rhys and Azriel still instructed me whenever they could, though I truly loved to fly, the thought of exposing sensitive wings to the cold made me shiver.

Few people recognized me while I strode by, my power firmly restrained within me, and most too concerned with decorating or enjoying the first snow to note those around them, anyway.

A small mercy, though I certainly didn't mind being approached. As High Lady, I hosted weekly open audiences with Rhys at the House of Wind. The requests ranged from the small—a faelight lamppost was broken—to the complicated—could we please stop importing goods from other courts because it impacted local artisans.

Some were issues Rhys had dealt with for centuries now, but he never acted like he had.

No, he listened to each petitioner, asked thorough questions, and then sent them on their way with a promise to send an answer to them soon. It had taken me a few sessions to get the hang of it—the questions he used, the *way* he listened. He hadn't pushed me to step in unless necessary, had granted me the space to figure out the rhythm and style of these audiences and begin asking questions of my own. And then begin writing replies to the petitioners, too. Rhys personally answered each and every one of them. And I now did, too.

Hence the ever-growing stacks of paperwork in so many rooms of the town house.

How he'd lasted so long without a team of secretaries assisting him, I had no idea.

But as I eased down the steep slope of the street, the bright-colored buildings of the Rainbow glowing around me like a shimmering memory of summer, I again mulled it over.

Velaris was by no means poor, its people mostly cared for, the buildings and streets well kept. My sister, it seemed, had managed to find the only thing relatively close to a slum. And insisted on living there, in a building that was older than Rhys and in dire need of repairs.

There were only a few blocks in the city like that. When I'd asked Rhys about them, about why they had not been improved, he merely said that he had tried. But displacing people while their homes were torn down and rebuilt . . . Tricky.

I hadn't been surprised two days ago when Rhys had handed me a piece of paper and asked if there was anything else I would like to add to it. On the paper had been a list of charities that he donated to around Solstice-time, everything from aiding the poor, sick, and elderly to grants for young mothers to start their own businesses. I'd added only two items, both to societies that I'd heard about through my own volunteering: donations to the humans displaced by the war with Hybern, as well as to Illyrian war widows and their families. The sums we allocated were sizable, more money than I'd ever dreamed of possessing.

Once, all I had wanted was enough food, money, and time to paint. Nothing more. I would have been content to let my sisters wed, to remain and care for my father.

But beyond my mate, my family, beyond being High Lady— the mere fact that I now lived *here*, that I could walk through an entire artists' quarter whenever I wished . . .

Another avenue bisected the street midway down its slope, and I turned onto it, the neat rows of houses and galleries and studios curving away into the snow. But even amongst the bright colors, there were patches of gray, of emptiness.

I approached one such hollow place, a half-crumbled building. Its mint-green paint had turned grayish, as if the very light had bled from the color as the building shattered. Indeed, the few buildings around it were also muted and cracked, a gallery across the street boarded up.

A few months ago, I'd begun donating a portion of my monthly salary—the idea of receiving such a thing was still utterly ludicrous—to rebuilding the Rainbow and helping its artists, but the scars remained, on both these buildings and their residents.

And the mound of snow-dusted rubble before me: who had dwelled there, worked there? Did they live, or had they been slaughtered in the attack?

There were many such places in Velaris. I'd seen them in my work, while handing out winter coats and meeting with families in their homes.

I blew out another breath. I knew I lingered too often, too long at such sites. I knew I should continue on, smiling as if nothing bothered me, as if all were well. And yet . . .

"They got out in time," a female voice said behind me.

I turned, boots slipping on the slick cobblestones. Throwing out a hand to steady me, I gripped the first thing I came into contact with: a fallen chunk of rock from the wrecked house.

But it was the sight of who, exactly, stood behind me, gazing at the rubble, that made me abandon any mortification.

I had not forgotten her in the months since the attack.

I had not forgotten the sight of her standing outside that shop door, a rusted pipe raised over one shoulder, squaring off against the gathered Hybern soldiers, ready to go down swinging for the terrified people huddled inside.

A faint rose blush glowed prettily on her pale green skin, her sable hair flowing past her chest. She was bundled against the cold in a brown coat, a pink scarf wrapped around her neck and lower half of her face, but her long, delicate fingers were gloveless as she crossed her arms.

Faerie—and not a kind I saw too frequently. Her face and body reminded me of the High Fae, though her ears were slenderer, longer than mine. Her form slimmer, sleeker, even with the heavy coat.

I met her eyes, a vibrant ochre that made me wonder what paints I'd have to blend and wield to capture their likeness, and offered a small smile. "I'm glad to hear it."

Silence fell, interrupted by the merry singing of a few people down the street and the wind gusting off the Sidra.

The faerie only inclined her head. "Lady."

I fumbled for words, for something High Lady–ish and yet accessible, and came up empty. Came up so empty that I blurted, "It's snowing."

As if the drifting veils of white could be anything else.

The faerie inclined her head again. "It is." She smiled at the sky, snow catching in her inky hair. "A fine first snow at that."

I surveyed the ruin behind me. "You—you know the people who lived here?"

"I did. They're living at a relative's farm in the lowlands now." She waved a hand toward the distant sea, to the flat expanse of land between Velaris and the shore.

"Ah," I managed to say, then jerked my chin at the boarded-up shop across the street. "What about that one?"

The faerie surveyed where I'd indicated. Her mouth—painted a berry pink—tightened. "Not so happy an ending, I'm afraid."

My palms turned sweaty within my wool gloves. "I see."

She faced me again, silken hair flowing around her. "Her name was Polina. That was her gallery. For centuries."

Now it was a dark, quiet husk.

"I'm sorry," I said, uncertain what else to offer.

The faerie's slim, dark brows narrowed. "Why should you be?" She added, "My lady."

I gnawed on my lip. Discussing such things with strangers . . . Perhaps not a good idea. So I ignored her question and asked, "Does she have any family?" I hoped they'd made it, at least.

"They live out in the lowlands, too. Her sister and nieces and nephews." The faerie again studied the boarded-up front. "It's for sale now."

I blinked, grasping the implied offer. "Oh—oh, I wasn't asking after it for *that* reason." It hadn't even entered my mind.

"Why not?"

A frank, easy question. Perhaps more direct than most people, certainly strangers, dared to be with me. "I—what use would I have for it?"

She gestured to me with a hand, the motion effortlessly graceful. "Rumor has it that you're a fine artist. I can think of many uses for the space."

I glanced away, hating myself a bit for it. "I'm not in the market, I'm afraid."

The faerie shrugged with one shoulder. "Well, whether you are or aren't, you needn't go skulking around here. Every door is open to you, you know."

"As High Lady?" I dared ask.

"As one of us," she said simply.

The words settled in, strange and yet like a piece I had not known was missing. An offered hand I had not realized how badly I wanted to grasp.

"I'm Feyre," I said, removing my glove and extending my arm.

The faerie clasped my fingers, her grip steel-strong despite her slender build. "Ressina." Not someone prone to excessive smiling, but still full of a practical sort of warmth.

Noon bells chimed in a tower at the edge of the Rainbow, the sound soon echoed across the city in the other sister-towers.

"I should be going," I said, releasing Ressina's hand and retreating a step. "It was nice to meet you." I tugged my glove back on, my fingers already stinging with cold. Perhaps I'd take some time this winter to master my fire gifts more precisely. Learning how to warm clothes and skin without burning myself would be mighty helpful.

Ressina pointed to a building down the street—across the intersection I had just passed through. The same building she'd defended, its walls painted raspberry pink, and doors and windows a bright turquoise, like the water around Adriata. "I'm one of the artists who uses that studio space over there. If you ever want a guide, or even some company, I'm there most days. I live above the studio." An elegant wave toward the tiny round windows on the second level.

I put a hand on my chest. "Thank you."

Again that silence, and I took in that shop, the doorway Ressina had stood before, guarding her home and others.

"We remember it, you know," Ressina said quietly, drawing my stare away. But her attention had landed on the rubble behind us, on the boarded-up studio, on the street, as if she, too, could see through the snow to the blood that had run between the cobble-stones. "That you came for us that day."

I didn't know what to do with my body, my hands, so I opted for stillness.

Ressina met my stare at last, her ochre eyes bright. "We keep away to let you have your privacy, but don't think for one moment that there isn't a single one of us who doesn't know and remember, who isn't grateful that you came here and fought for us."

It hadn't been enough, even so. The ruined building behind me was proof of that. People had still died.

Ressina took a few unhurried steps toward her studio, then stopped. "There's a group of us who paint together at my studio. One night a week. We're meeting in two days' time. It would be an honor if you joined us."

"What sort of things do you paint?" My question was soft as the snow falling past us.

Ressina smiled slightly. "The things that need telling."

✢

Even with the icy evening soon descending upon Velaris, people packed the streets, laden with bags and boxes, some lugging enor-mous fruit baskets from one of the many stands now occupying either Palace.

My fur-lined hood shielding me against the cold, I browsed through the vendor carts and storefronts in the Palace of Thread and Jewels, surveying the latter, mostly.

Some of the public areas remained heated, but enough of Velaris had now been temporarily left exposed to the bitter wind that I wished I'd opted for a heavier sweater that morning. Learning how to warm myself without summoning a flame would be handy indeed. If I ever had the time to do it.

I was circling back to a display in one of the shops built beneath the overhanging buildings when an arm looped through mine and Mor drawled, "Amren would love you forever if you bought her a sapphire that big."

I laughed, tugging back my hood enough to see her fully. Mor's cheeks were flushed against the cold, her braided golden hair spilling into the white fur lining her cloak. "Unfortunately, I don't think our coffers would return the feeling."

Mor smirked. "You *do* know that we're well-off, don't you? You could fill a bathtub with those things"—she jerked her chin toward the egg-sized sapphire in the window of the jewelry shop—"and barely make a dent in our accounts."

I knew. I'd seen the lists of assets. I still couldn't wrap my mind around the enormity of Rhys's wealth. *My* wealth. It didn't feel real, those numbers and figures. Like it was children's play money. I only bought what I needed.

But now . . . "I'm looking for something to get her for Solstice."

Mor surveyed the lineup of jewels, both uncut and set, in the window. Some gleamed like fallen stars. Others smoldered, as if they had been carved from the burning heart of the earth. "Amren does deserve a decent present this year, doesn't she?"

After what Amren had done during that final battle to destroy Hybern's armies, the choice she'd made to remain here . . . "We all do."

Mor nudged me with an elbow, though her brown eyes gleamed. "And will Varian be joining us, do you think?"

I snorted. "When I asked her yesterday, she hedged."

"I think that means yes. Or he'll at least be visiting *her*."

I smiled at the thought, and pulled Mor along to the next display window, pressing against her side for warmth. Amren and the Prince of Adriata hadn't officially declared anything, but I sometimes dreamed of it, too—that moment when she had shed her immortal skin and Varian had fallen to his knees.

A creature of flame and brimstone, built in another world to mete out a cruel god's judgment, to be his executioner upon the masses of helpless mortals. Fifteen thousand years, she had been stuck in this world.

And had not loved, not in the way that could alter history, alter fate, until that silver-haired Prince of Adriata. Or at least loved in the way that Amren was capable of loving anything.

So, yes: nothing was declared between them. But I knew he visited her, secretly, in this city. Mostly because some mornings, Amren would strut into the town house smirking like a cat.

But for what she'd been willing to walk away from, so that we could be saved . . .

Mor and I spied the piece in the window at the same moment. "That one," she declared.

I was already moving for the glass front door, a silver bell ringing merrily as we entered.

The shopkeeper was wide-eyed but beaming as we pointed to the piece, and swiftly laid it out on a black velvet pad. She made a sweet-tempered excuse to retrieve something from the back, granting us privacy to examine it as we stood before the polished wood counter.

"It's perfect," Mor breathed, the stones fracturing the light and burning with their own inner fire.

I ran a finger over the cool silver settings. "What do *you* want as a present?"

Mor shrugged, her heavy brown coat bringing out the rich soil of her eyes. "I've got everything I need."

"Try telling Rhys that. He says Solstice isn't about getting gifts you *need*, but rather ones you'd never buy for yourself." Mor rolled her eyes. Even though I was inclined to do the same, I pushed, "So what *do* you want?"

She ran a finger along a cut stone. "Nothing. I—there's nothing I want."

Beyond things she perhaps was not ready to ask for, search for.

I again examined the piece and casually asked, "You've been at Rita's a great deal lately. Is there anyone you might want to bring to Solstice dinner?"

Mor's eyes sliced to mine. "No."

It was her business, when and how to inform the others what she'd told me during the war. When and how to tell Azriel especially.

My only role in it was to stand by her—to have her back when she needed it.

So I went on, "What are *you* getting the others?"

She scowled. "After centuries of gifts, it's a pain in my ass to find something new for all of them. I'm fairly certain Azriel has a drawer full of all the daggers I've bought him throughout the centuries that he's too polite to throw away, but won't ever use."

"You honestly think he'd ever give up Truth-Teller?"

"He gave it to Elain," Mor said, admiring a moonstone necklace in the counter's glass case.

"She gave it back," I amended, failing to block out the image of the black blade piercing through the King of Hybern's throat. But

Elain *had* given it back—had pressed it into Azriel's hands after the battle, just as he had pressed it into hers before. And then walked away without looking back.

Mor hummed to herself. The jeweler returned a moment later, and I signed the purchase to my personal credit account, trying not to cringe at the enormous sum of money that just disappeared with a stroke of a golden pen.

"Speaking of Illyrian warriors," I said as we strode into the crammed Palace square and edged around a red-painted cart selling cups of piping hot molten chocolate, "what the hell *do* I get either of them?"

I didn't have the nerve to ask what I should get for Rhys, since, even though I adored Mor, it felt *wrong* to ask another person for advice on what to buy my mate.

"You *could* honestly get Cassian a new knife and he'd kiss you for it. But Az would probably prefer no presents at all, just to avoid the attention while opening it."

I laughed. "True."

Arm in arm, we continued on, the aromas of roasting hazelnuts, pine cones, and chocolate replacing the usual salt-and-lemon-verbena scent that filled the city. "Do you plan to visit Viviane during Solstice?"

In the months since the war had ended, Mor had remained in contact with the Lady of the Winter Court, perhaps soon to be *High* Lady, if Viviane had anything to do about it. They'd been friends for centuries, until Amarantha's reign had severed contact, and though the war with Hybern had been brutal, one of the good things to come of it had been the rekindling of their friendship. Rhys and Kallias had a still-lukewarm alliance, but it seemed

Mor's relationship with the High Lord of Winter's mate would be the bridge between our two courts.

My friend smiled warmly. "Perhaps a day or two after. Their celebrating lasts for a whole week."

"Have you been before?"

A shake of her head, golden hair catching in the faelight lamps. "No. They usually keep their borders closed, even to friends. But with Kallias now in power, and especially with Viviane at his side, they're starting to open up once more."

"I can only imagine their celebrations."

Her eyes glowed. "Viviane told me about them once. They make ours look positively dull. Dancing and drinking, feasting and gifting. Roaring fires made from entire tree trunks and cauldrons full of mulled wine, the singing of a thousand minstrels flowing throughout their palace, answered by the bells ringing on the large sleighs pulled by those beautiful white bears." She sighed. I echoed it, the image she'd crafted hovering in the frosty air between us.

Here in Velaris, we would celebrate the longest night of the year. In Kallias's territory, it seemed, they would celebrate the winter itself.

Mor's smile faded. "I did find you for a reason, you know."

"Not just to shop?"

She nudged me with an elbow. "We're to head to the Hewn City tonight."

I cringed. "*We* as in all of us?"

"You, me, and Rhys, at least."

I bit back a groan. "Why?"

Mor paused at a vendor, examining the neatly folded scarves

displayed. "Tradition. Around Solstice, we make a little visit to the Court of Nightmares to wish them well."

"Really?"

Mor grimaced, nodding to the vendor and continuing on. "As I said, tradition. To foster goodwill. Or as much of it as we have. And after the battles this summer, it wouldn't hurt."

Keir and his Darkbringer army had fought, after all.

We eased through the densely packed heart of the Palace, passing beneath a latticework of faelights just beginning to twinkle awake overhead. From a slumbering, quiet place inside me, the painting name flitted by. *Frost and Starlight.*

"So you and Rhys decided to tell me mere hours before we go?"

"Rhys has been away all day. *I* decided that we're to go tonight. Since we don't want to ruin the actual Solstice by visiting, now is best."

There were plenty of days between now and Solstice Eve to do it. But Mor's face remained carefully casual.

I still pushed, "You preside over the Hewn City, and deal with them all the time." She as good as ruled over it when Rhys wasn't there. And handled her awful father plenty.

Mor sensed the question within my statement. "Eris will be there tonight. I heard it from Az this morning."

I remained quiet, waiting.

Mor's brown eyes darkened. "I want to see for myself just how cozy he and my father have become."

It was good enough reason for me.

CHAPTER
5

Feyre

I was curled up on the bed, toasty and drowsy atop the layers of blankets and down quilts, when Rhys finally returned home as dusk fell.

I felt his power beckoning to me long before he got near the house, a dark melody through the world.

Mor had announced we wouldn't be going to the Hewn City for another hour or so, long enough that I'd forgone touching that paperwork on the rosewood writing desk across the room and had instead picked up a book. I'd barely managed ten pages before Rhys opened the bedroom door.

His Illyrian leathers gleamed with melted snow, and more of it shone on his dark hair and wings as he quietly shut the door. "Right where I left you."

I smiled, setting down the book beside me. It was nearly swallowed by the ivory down duvet. "Isn't this all I'm good for?"

A rogue smile tugging up one corner of his mouth, Rhys began removing his weapons, then the clothes. But despite the humor lighting his eyes, each movement was heavy and slow—as if he fought exhaustion with every breath.

"Maybe we should tell Mor to delay the meeting at the Court of Nightmares." I frowned.

He shucked off his jacket, the leathers thumping as they landed on the desk chair. "Why? If Eris will indeed be there, I'd like to surprise him with a little visit of my own."

"You look exhausted, that's why."

He put a dramatic hand over his heart. "Your concern warms me more than any winter fire, my love."

I rolled my eyes and sat up. "Did you at least eat?"

He shrugged, his dark shirt straining across his broad shoulders. "I'm fine." His gaze slid over my bare legs as I pushed back the covers.

Heat bloomed in me, but I shoved my feet into slippers. "I'll get you food."

"I don't want—"

"When did you last eat?"

A sullen silence.

"I thought so." I hauled a fleece-lined robe around my shoulders. "Wash up and change. We're leaving in forty minutes. I'll be back soon."

He tucked in his wings, the faelight gilding the talon atop each one. "You don't need to—"

"I want to, and I'm going to." With that, I was out the door and padding down the cerulean-blue hallway.

Five minutes later, Rhys held the door open for me wearing nothing but his undershorts as I strode in, tray in my hands.

"Considering that you brought the entire damn kitchen," he

mused as I headed for the desk, still not anywhere near dressed for our visit, "I should have just gone downstairs."

I stuck out my tongue, but scowled as I scanned the cluttered desk for any spare space. None. Even the small table by the window was covered with things. All important, vital things. I made do with the bed.

Rhys sat, folding his wings behind him before reaching to pull me into his lap, but I dodged his hands and kept a healthy distance away. "Eat the food first."

"Then I'll eat you after," he countered, grinning wickedly, but tore into the food.

The rate and intensity of that eating was enough to bank any rising heat in me at his words. "Did you eat *at all* today?"

A flash of violet eyes as he finished off his bread and began on the cold roast beef. "I had an apple this morning."

"Rhys."

"I was busy."

"*Rhys.*"

He set down his fork, his mouth twitching toward a smile. "Feyre."

I crossed my arms. "No one is too busy to eat."

"You're fussing."

"It's my job to fuss. And besides, *you* fuss plenty. Over far more trivial things."

"Your cycle *isn't* trivial."

"I was in a *little* bit of pain—"

"You were thrashing on the bed as if someone had gutted you."

"And *you* were acting like an overbearing mother hen."

"I didn't see you screaming at Cassian, Mor, or Az when *they* expressed concern for you."

"They didn't try to spoon-feed me like an invalid!"

Rhys chuckled, finishing off his food. "I'll eat regular meals if you allow me to turn into an overbearing mother hen twice a year."

Right—because my cycle was so different in this body. Gone were the monthly discomforts. I'd thought it a gift.

Until two months ago. When the first one had happened.

In place of those monthly, human discomforts was a biannual week of stomach-shredding *agony*. Even Madja, Rhys's favored healer, could do little for the pain short of rendering me unconscious. There had been a point during that week when I'd debated it, the pain slicing from my back and stomach down to my thighs, up to my arms, like living bands of lightning flashing through me. My cycle had never been pleasant as a human, and there had indeed been days when I couldn't get out of bed. It seemed that in being Made, the amplification of my attributes hadn't stopped at strength and Fae features. Not at all.

Mor had little to offer me beyond commiseration and ginger tea. At least it was only twice a year, she'd consoled me. That was two times too many, I'd managed to groan to her.

Rhys had stayed with me the entire time, stroking my hair, replacing the heated blankets that I soaked with sweat, even helping me clean myself off. Blood was blood, was all he said when I'd objected to him seeing me peel off the soiled undergarments. I'd been barely able to move at that point without whimpering, so the words hadn't entirely sunken in.

Along with the implication of that blood. At least the contraceptive brew he took was working. But conceiving amongst the Fae was rare and difficult enough that I sometimes wondered if waiting until I was ready for children might wind up biting me in the ass.

I hadn't forgotten the Bone Carver's vision, how he'd appeared to me. I knew Rhys hadn't, either.

But he hadn't pushed, or asked. I'd once told him that I wanted to live with him, experience *life* with him, before we had children. I still held to that. There was so much to do, our days too busy to even *think* about bringing a child into the world, my life full enough that even though it would be a blessing beyond measure, I would endure the twice-a-year agony for the time being. And help my sisters with them, too.

Fae fertility cycles had never been something I'd considered, and explaining them to Nesta and Elain had been uncomfortable, to say the least.

Nesta had only stared at me in that unblinking, cold way. Elain had blushed, muttering about the impropriety of such things. But they had been Made nearly six months ago. It was coming. Soon. If being Made somehow didn't interfere with it.

I'd have to find some way to convince Nesta to send word when hers started. Like hell would I allow her to endure that pain alone. I wasn't sure she *could* endure that pain alone.

Elain, at least, would be too polite to send Lucien away when he wanted to help. She was too polite to send him away on a normal day. She just ignored him or barely spoke to him until he got the hint and left. As far as I knew, he hadn't come within touching distance since the aftermath of that final battle. No, she tended to her gardens here, silently mourning her lost human life. Mourning Graysen.

How Lucien withstood it, I didn't know. Not that he'd shown any interest in bridging that gap between them.

"Where did you go?" Rhys asked, draining his wine and setting aside the tray.

If I wanted to talk, he'd listen. If I didn't want to, he would let it go. It had been our unspoken bargain from the start—to listen when the other needed, and give space when it was required. He was still slowly working his way through telling me all that had been done to him, all he'd witnessed Under the Mountain. There were still nights when I'd kiss away his tears, one by one.

This subject, however, was not so difficult to discuss. "I was thinking about Elain," I said, leaning against the edge of the desk. "And Lucien."

Rhys arched a brow, and I told him.

When I finished, his face was contemplative. "Will Lucien be joining us for the Solstice?"

"Is it bad if he does?"

Rhys let out a hum, his wings tucking in further. I had no idea how he withstood the cold while flying, even with a shield. Whenever I'd tried these past few weeks, I'd barely lasted more than a few minutes. The only time I'd managed had been last week, when our flight from the House of Wind had turned far warmer.

Rhys said at last, "I can stomach being around him."

"I'm sure he'd love to hear that thrilling endorsement."

A half smile that had me walking toward him, stopping between his legs. He braced his hands idly on my hips. "I can let go of the taunts," he said, scanning my face. "And the fact that he still harbors some hope of one day reuniting with Tamlin. But I cannot let go of how he treated you after Under the Mountain."

"I can. I've forgiven him for that."

"Well, you'll forgive *me* if I can't." Icy rage darkened the stars in those violet eyes.

"You still can barely talk to Nesta," I said. "Yet Elain you can talk to nicely."

"Elain is Elain."

"If you blame one, you have to blame the other."

"No, I don't. Elain is Elain," he repeated. "Nesta is . . . she's Illyrian. I mean that as a compliment, but she's an Illyrian at heart. So there is no excuse for her behavior."

"She more than made up for it this summer, Rhys."

"I cannot forgive anyone who made you suffer."

Cold, brutal words, spoken with such casual grace.

But he still didn't care about those who'd made *him* suffer. I ran a hand over the swirls and whorls of tattoos across his muscled chest, tracing the intricate lines. He shuddered under my fingers, wings twitching. "They're my family. You have to forgive Nesta at some point."

He rested his brow against my chest, right between my breasts, and wrapped his arms around my waist. For a long minute, he only breathed in the scent of me, as if taking it deep into his lungs. "Should that be my Solstice gift to you?" he murmured. "Forgiving Nesta for letting her fourteen-year-old sister go into those woods?"

I hooked a finger under his chin and tugged his head up. "You won't get any Solstice gift at all from *me* if you keep up this nonsense."

A wicked grin.

"Prick," I hissed, making to step back, but his arms tightened around me.

We fell silent, just staring at each other. Then Rhys said down the bond, *A thought for a thought, Feyre darling?*

I smiled at the request, the old game between us. But it faded as I answered, *I went into the Rainbow today.*

Oh? He nuzzled the plane of my stomach.

I dragged my hands through his dark hair, savoring the silken

51

strands against my calluses. *There's an artist, Ressina. She invited me to come paint with her and some others in two nights.*

Rhys pulled back to scan my face, then arched a brow. "Why do you not sound excited about it?"

I gestured to our room, the town house, and blew out a breath. "I haven't painted anything in a while."

Not since we'd returned from battle. Rhys remained quiet, letting me sort through the jumble of words inside me.

"It feels selfish," I admitted. "To take the time, when there is so much to do and—"

"It is not selfish." His hands tightened on my hips. "If you want to paint, then paint, Feyre."

"People in this city still don't have homes."

"You taking a few hours every day to paint won't change that."

"It's not just that." I leaned down until my brow rested on his, the citrus-and-sea scent of him filling my lungs, my heart. "There are too many of them—things I want to paint. Need to. Picking one . . ." I took an unsteady breath and pulled back. "I'm not quite certain I'm ready to see what emerges when I paint some of them."

"Ah." He traced soothing, loving lines down my back. "Whether you join them this week, or two months from now, I think you should go. Try it out." He surveyed the room, the thick rug, as if he could see the entire town house beneath. "We can turn your old bedroom into a studio, if you want—"

"It's fine," I cut him off. "It—the light isn't ideal in there." At his raised brows, I admitted, "I checked. The only room that's good for it is the sitting room, and I'd rather not fill up the house with the reek of paint."

"I don't think anyone would mind."

"*I'd* mind. And I like privacy, anyway. The last thing I want is Amren standing behind me, critiquing my work as I go."

Rhys chuckled. "Amren can be dealt with."

"I'm not sure you and I are talking about the same Amren, then."

He grinned, tugging me close again, and murmured against my stomach, "It's your birthday on Solstice."

"So?" I'd been trying to forget that fact. And let the others forget it, too.

Rhys's smile became subdued—feline. "So, that means you get *two* presents."

I groaned. "I never should have told you."

"You were born on the longest night of the year." His fingers again stroked down my back. Lower. "You were meant to be at my side from the very beginning."

He traced the seam of my backside with a long, lazy stroke. With me standing before him like this, he could instantly smell the shift in my scent as my core heated.

I managed to say down the bond before words failed me, *Your turn. A thought for a thought.*

He pressed a kiss to my stomach, right over my navel. "Have I told you about that first time you winnowed and tackled me into the snow?"

I smacked his shoulder, the muscle beneath hard as stone. "*That's* your thought for a thought?"

He smiled against my stomach, his fingers still exploring, coaxing. "You tackled me like an Illyrian. Perfect form, a direct hit. But then you lay on top of me, panting. All I wanted to do was get us both naked."

"Why am I not surprised?" Yet I threaded my fingers through his hair.

The fabric of my dressing gown was barely more than cobwebs between us as he huffed a laugh onto my belly. I hadn't bothered putting on anything beneath. "You drove me out of my mind. All those months. I still don't quite believe I get to have this. Have you."

My throat tightened. That was the thought he wanted to trade, needed to share. "I wanted you, even Under the Mountain," I said softly. "I chalked it up to those horrible circumstances, but after we killed her, when I couldn't tell anyone how I felt—about how truly bad things were, I still told you. I've always been able to talk to you. I think my heart knew you were mine long before I ever realized it."

His eyes gleamed, and he buried his face between my breasts again, hands caressing my back. "I love you," he breathed. "More than life, more than my territory, more than my crown."

I knew. He'd given up that life to reforge the Cauldron, the fabric of the world itself, so I might survive. I hadn't had it in me to be furious with him about it afterward, or in the months since. He'd lived—it was a gift I would never stop being grateful for. And in the end, though, we'd saved each other. All of us had.

I kissed the top of his head. "I love you," I whispered onto his blue-black hair.

Rhys's hands clamped on the back of my thighs, the only warning before he smoothly twisted us, pinning me to the bed as he nuzzled my neck. "A week," he said onto my skin, gracefully folding his wings behind him. "A week to have you in this bed. That's all I want for Solstice."

I laughed breathlessly, but he flexed his hips, driving against me, the barriers between us little more than scraps of cloth. He brushed a kiss against my mouth, his wings a dark wall behind his shoulders. "You think I'm joking."

"We're strong for High Fae," I mused, fighting to concentrate as he tugged on my earlobe with his teeth, "but a week straight of sex? I don't think I'd be able to walk. Or you'd be able to function, at least with your favorite part."

He nipped the delicate arch of my ear, and my toes curled. "Then you'll just have to kiss my favorite part and make it better."

I slid a hand to that favorite part—*my* favorite part—and gripped him through his undershorts. He groaned, pressing himself into my touch, and the garment disappeared, leaving only my palm against the velvet hardness of him.

"We need to get dressed," I managed to say, even as my hand stroked over him.

"Later," he ground out, sucking on my lower lip.

Indeed. Rhys pulled back, tattooed arms braced on either side of my head. One was covered with his Illyrian markings, the other with the twin tattoo to the one on my arms: the last bargain we'd made. To remain together through all that waited ahead.

My core pounded, sister to my thunderous heartbeat, the need to have him buried inside me, to have him—

As if in mockery of those twin beats within me, a knocking rattled the bedroom door. "Just so you're aware," Mor chirped from the other side, "we *do* have to go soon."

Rhys let out a low growl that skittered over my skin, his hair slipping over his brow as he turned his head toward the door. Nothing but predatory intent in his glazed eyes. "We have thirty minutes," he said with remarkable smoothness.

"And it takes you two hours to get dressed," Mor quipped through the door. A sly pause. "And I'm not talking about Feyre."

Rhys grumbled a laugh and lowered his brow against mine. I closed my eyes, breathing him in, even while my fingers unfurled from around him. "This isn't finished," he promised me, his voice rough, before he kissed the hollow of my throat and pulled away. "Go terrorize someone else," he called to Mor, rolling his neck as his wings vanished and he stalked for the bathing room. "I need to primp."

Mor chuckled, her light footsteps soon fading away.

I slumped against the pillows and breathed deep, cooling the need that coursed through me. Water gurgled in the bathing room, followed by a soft yelp.

I wasn't the only one in need of cooling, it seemed.

Indeed, when I strode into the bathing room a few minutes later, Rhys was still cringing as he washed himself in the tub.

A dip of my fingers into the soapy water confirmed my suspicions: it was ice-cold.

CHAPTER
6

Morrigan

There was no light in this place.

There never had been.

Even the evergreen garlands, holly wreaths, and crackling birch-wood fires in honor of the Solstice couldn't pierce the eternal darkness that dwelled in the Hewn City.

It was not the sort of darkness that Mor had come to love in Velaris, the sort of darkness that was as much a part of Rhys as his blood.

It was the darkness of rotting things, of decay. The smothering darkness that withered all life.

And the golden-haired male standing before her in the throne room, amongst the towering pillars carved with those scaled, slithering beasts—he had been created from it. Thrived in it.

"I apologize if we interrupted your festivities," Rhysand purred to him. To Keir. And to the male beside him.

Eris.

The throne room was empty now. A word from Feyre, and the

usual ilk who dined and danced and schemed here were gone, leaving only Keir and the High Lord of Autumn's eldest son.

The former spoke first, adjusting the lapels on his black jacket. "To what do we owe this pleasure?"

The sneering tone. She could still hear the hissed insults beneath it, whispered long ago in her family's private suite, whispered at every meeting and gathering when her cousin was not present. *Half-breed monstrosity. A disgrace to the bloodline.*

"High Lord."

The words came out of her without thought. And her voice, the voice she used here . . . Not her own. Never her own, never down here with them in the darkness. Mor kept her voice just as cold and unforgiving as she corrected, "To what do we owe this pleasure, *High Lord.*"

She didn't bother to keep her teeth from flashing.

Keir ignored her.

His preferred method of insult: to act as if a person weren't worth the breath it'd take to speak with them.

Try something new, you miserable bastard.

Rhys cut in before Mor could contemplate saying just that, his dark power filling the room, the mountain, "We came, of course, to wish you and yours well for the Solstice. But it seems you already had a guest to entertain."

Az's information had been flawless, as it always was. When he'd found her reading up on Winter Court customs in the House of Wind's library this morning, she hadn't asked *how* he'd learned that Eris was to come tonight. She'd long since learned that Az was just as likely not to tell her.

But the Autumn Court male standing beside Keir . . . Mor made herself look at Eris. Into his amber eyes.

Colder than any hall of Kallias's court. They had been that way from the moment she'd met him, five centuries ago.

Eris laid a pale hand on the breast of his pewter-colored jacket, the portrait of Autumn Court gallantry. "I thought I'd extend some Solstice greetings of my own."

That voice. That silky, arrogant voice. It had not altered, not in tone or timbre, in the passing centuries, either. Had not changed since that day.

Warm, buttery sunlight through the leaves, setting them glowing like rubies and citrines. The damp, earthen scent of rotting things beneath the leaves and roots she lay upon. Had been thrown and left upon.

Everything hurt. Everything. She couldn't move. Couldn't do anything but watch the sun drift through the rich canopy far overhead, listen to the wind between the silvery trunks.

And the center of that pain, radiating outward like living fire with each uneven, rasping breath . . .

Light, steady steps crunched on the leaves. Six sets. A border guard, a patrol.

Help. Someone to help—

A male voice, foreign and deep, swore. Then went silent.

Went silent as a single pair of steps approached. She couldn't turn her head, couldn't bear the agony. Could do nothing but inhale each wet, shuddering breath.

"Don't touch her."

Those steps stopped.

It was not a warning to protect her. Defend her.

She knew the voice that spoke. Had dreaded hearing it.

She felt him approach now. Felt each reverberation in the leaves, the moss, the roots. As if the very land shuddered before him.

"No one touches her," he said. Eris. "The moment we do, she's our responsibility."

Cold, unfeeling words.

"But—but they nailed *a—"*

"No one touches her."

Nailed.

They had spiked nails into her.

Had pinned her down as she screamed, pinned her down as she roared at them, then begged them. And then they had taken out those long, brutal iron nails. And the hammer.

Three of them.

Three strikes of the hammer, drowned out by her screaming, by the pain.

She began shaking, hating it as much as she'd hated the begging. Her body bellowed in agony, those nails in her abdomen relentless.

A pale, beautiful face appeared above her, blocking out the jewel-like leaves above. Unmoved. Impassive. "I take it you do not wish to live here, Morrigan."

She would rather die here, bleed out here. She would rather die and return—return as something wicked and cruel, and shred them all apart.

He must have read it in her eyes. A small smile curved his lips. "I thought so."

Eris straightened, turning. Her fingers curled in the leaves and loamy soil.

She wished she could grow claws—grow claws as Rhys could—and rip out that pale throat. But that was not her gift. Her gift . . . her gift had left her here. Broken and bleeding.

Eris took a step away.

Someone behind him blurted, "We can't just leave her to—"

"We can, and we will," Eris said simply, his pace unfaltering as he strode away. "She chose to sully herself; her family chose to deal with her like garbage. I have already told them my decision in this matter."
A long pause, crueler than the rest. "And I am not in the habit of fucking Illyrian leftovers."

She couldn't stop it, then. The tears that slid out, hot and burning.

Alone. They would leave her alone here. Her friends did not know where she had gone. She barely knew where she was.

"But—" That dissenting voice cut in again.

"Move out."

There was no dissension after that.

And when their steps faded away, then vanished, the silence returned.

The sun and the wind and the leaves.

The blood and the iron and the soil beneath her nails.

The pain.

A subtle nudge of Feyre's hand against her own drew her out, away from that bloody clearing just over the border of the Autumn Court.

Mor threw her High Lady a grateful glance, which Feyre smartly ignored, already returning her attention to the conversation. Never having taken her focus off it in the first place.

Feyre had fallen into the role of mistress of this horrible city with far more ease than she had. Clad in a sparkling onyx gown, the crescent-moon diadem atop her head, her friend looked every part the imperious ruler. As much a part of this place as the twining, serpentine beasts carved and etched everywhere. What Keir, perhaps, had one day pictured for Mor herself.

Not the red gown Mor wore, bright and bold, or the gold

jewelry at her wrists, her ears, shimmering like sunlight down here in the gloom.

"If you wanted this little liaison to remain private," Rhys was saying with lethal calm, "perhaps a public gathering was not the wisest place to meet."

Indeed.

The Steward of the Hewn City waved a hand. "Why should we have anything to hide? After the war, we're all such good friends."

She often dreamed of gutting him. Sometimes with a knife; sometimes with her own bare hands.

"And how does your father's court fare, Eris?" A mild, bored question from Feyre.

His amber eyes held nothing but distaste.

A roaring filled Mor's head at that look. She could barely hear his drawled answer. Or Rhys's reply.

It had once been her delight to taunt Keir and this court, to keep them on their toes. Hell, she'd even snapped a few of the Steward's bones this spring—after Rhys had shattered his arms into uselessness. Had been glad to do it, after what Keir had said to Feyre, and then delighted when her mother had banished her from their private quarters. An order that still held. But from the moment Eris had walked into that council chamber all those months ago . . .

You are over five hundred years old, she often reminded herself. She could face it, handle it better than this.

I am not in the habit of fucking Illyrian leftovers.

Even now, even after Azriel had found her in those woods, after Madja had healed her until no trace of those nails marred her stomach . . . She should not have come here tonight.

Her skin became tight, her stomach roiling. *Coward.*

She had faced down enemies, fought in many wars, and yet this, these two males together—

Mor felt more than saw Feyre stiffen beside her at something Eris had said.

Her High Lady answered Eris, "Your father is forbidden to cross into the human lands." No room for compromise with that tone, with the steel in Feyre's eyes.

Eris only shrugged. "I don't think it's your call."

Rhys slid his hands into his pockets, the portrait of casual grace. Yet the shadows and star-flecked darkness that wafted from him, that set the mountain shuddering beneath his every step—that was the true face of the High Lord of the Night Court. The most powerful High Lord in history. "I would suggest reminding Beron that territory expansion is not on the table. For any court."

Eris wasn't fazed. Nothing had ever disturbed him, ruffled him. Mor had hated it from the moment she'd met him—that distance, that coldness. That lack of interest or feeling for the world. "Then I would suggest to you, High Lord, that you speak to your dear friend Tamlin about it."

"Why." Feyre's question was sharp as a blade.

Eris's mouth curved in an adder's smile. "Because Tamlin's territory is the only one that borders the human lands. I'd think that anyone looking to expand would have to go through the Spring Court first. Or at least obtain his permission."

Another person she'd one day kill. If Feyre and Rhys didn't do it first.

It didn't matter what Tamlin had done in the war, if he'd brought Beron and the human forces with him. If he'd played Hybern.

It was another day, another female lying on the ground, that Mor would not forget, could not forgive.

Rhys's cold face turned contemplative, though. She could easily read the reluctance in his eyes, the annoyance at having Eris tip him off, but information was information.

Mor glanced toward Keir and found him watching her.

Save for her initial order to the Steward, she had not spoken a word. Contributed to this meeting. Stepped up.

She could see that in Keir's eyes. The satisfaction.

Say something. Think of something to say. To strip him down to nothing.

But Rhys deemed they were done, linking his arm through Feyre's and guiding them away, the mountain indeed trembling beneath their steps. What he'd said to Eris, Mor had no idea.

Pathetic. Cowardly and pathetic.

Truth is your gift. Truth is your curse.

Say something.

But the words to strike down her father did not come.

Her red gown flowing behind her, Mor turned her back on him, on the smirking heir to Autumn, and followed her High Lord and Lady through the darkness and back into the light.

CHAPTER
7

Rhysand

"You really do know how to give Solstice presents, Az."

I turned from the wall of windows in my private study at the House of Wind, Velaris awash in the hues of early morning.

My spymaster and brother remained on the other side of the sprawling oak desk, the maps and documents he'd presented littering the surface. His expression might as well have been stone. Had been that way from the moment he'd knocked on the double doors to the study just after dawn. As if he'd known that sleep had been futile for me last night after Eris's not-so-subtle warning about Tamlin and his borders.

Feyre hadn't mentioned it when we'd returned home. Hadn't seemed ready to discuss it: how to deal with the High Lord of Spring. She'd quickly fallen asleep, leaving me to brood before the fire in the sitting room.

It was little wonder I'd flown up here before sunrise, eager for the biting cold to chase the weight of the sleepless night away from me. My wings were still numb in spots from the flight.

"You wanted information," Az said mildly. At his side, Truth-Teller's obsidian hilt seemed to absorb the first rays of the sun.

I rolled my eyes, leaning against the desk and gesturing to what he'd compiled. "You couldn't have waited until after Solstice for this particular gem?"

One glance at Azriel's unreadable face and I added, "Don't bother to answer that."

A corner of Azriel's mouth curled up, the shadows about him sliding over his neck like living tattoos, twins to the Illyrian ones marked beneath his leathers.

Shadows different from anything my powers summoned, spoke to. Born in a lightless, airless prison meant to break him.

Instead, he had learned its language.

Though the cobalt Siphons were proof that his Illyrian heritage ran true, even the rich lore of that warrior-people, *my* warrior-people, did not have an explanation for where the shadowsinger gifts came from. They certainly weren't connected to the Siphons, to the raw killing power most Illyrians possessed and channeled through the stones to keep from destroying everything in its path. The bearer included.

Drawing my eyes from the stones atop his hands, I frowned at the stack of papers Az had presented moments ago. "Have you told Cassian?"

"I came right here," Azriel said. "He'll arrive soon enough, anyway."

I chewed on my lip as I studied the territory map of Illyria. "It's more clans than I expected," I admitted and sent a flock of shadows skittering across the room to soothe the power now stirring, restless, in my veins. "Even in my worst-case calculations."

"It's not every member of these clans," Az said, his grim face undermining his attempt to soften the blow. "This overall number just reflects the places where discontent is spreading, not where the majorities lie." He pointed with a scarred finger to one of the camps. "There are only two females here who seem to be spewing poison about the war. One a widow, and one a mother to a soldier."

"Where there's smoke, there's fire," I countered.

Azriel studied the map for a long minute. I gave him the silence, knowing that he'd speak only when he was damn well ready. As boys, Cassian and I had devoted hours to pummeling Az, trying to get him to speak. He'd never once yielded.

"The Illyrians are pieces of shit," he said too quietly.

I opened my mouth and shut it.

Shadows gathered around his wings, trailing off him and onto the thick red rug. "They train and train as warriors, and yet when they don't come home, their families make *us* into villains for sending them to war?"

"Their families have lost something irreplaceable," I said carefully.

Azriel waved a scarred hand, his cobalt Siphon glinting with the movement as his fingers cut through the air. "They're hypocrites."

"And what would you have me do, then? Disband the largest army in Prythian?"

Az didn't answer.

I held his gaze, though. Held that ice-cold stare that still sometimes scared the shit out of me. I'd seen what he'd done to his half brothers centuries ago. Still dreamed of it. The act itself wasn't what lingered. Every bit of it had been deserved. Every damn bit.

But it was the frozen precipice that Az had plummeted into that sometimes rose from the pit of my memory.

The beginnings of that frost cracked over his eyes now. So I said calmly, yet with little room for argument, "I am not going to disband the Illyrians. There is nowhere for them to go, anyway. And if we try to drag them out of those mountains, they might launch the very assault we're trying to defuse."

Az said nothing.

"But perhaps more pressing," I went on, jabbing a finger on the sprawling continent, "is the fact that the human queens have not returned to their own territories. They linger in that joint palace of theirs. Beyond that, Hybern's general populace is not too thrilled to have lost this war. And with the wall gone, who knows what other Fae territories might make a grab for human lands?" My jaw tightened at that last one. "This peace is tenuous."

"I know that," Az said at last.

"So we might need the Illyrians again before it is over. Need them willing to shed blood."

Feyre knew. I'd been filling her in on every report and meeting. But this latest one . . . "We will keep an eye on the dissenters," I finished, letting Az sense a rumble of the power that prowled inside me, let him *feel* that I meant every word. "Cassian knows it's growing amongst the camps and is willing to do whatever it takes to fix it."

"He doesn't know just how many there are."

"And perhaps we should wait to tell him. Until after the holiday." Az blinked. I explained quietly, "He's going to have enough to deal with. Let him enjoy the holiday while he can."

Az and I made a point not to mention Nesta. Not amongst each other, and certainly not in front of Cassian. I didn't let myself contemplate it, either. Neither did Mor, given her unusual silence on the matter since the war had ended.

"He'll be pissed at us for keeping it from him."

"He already suspects much of it, so it's only confirmation at this point."

Az ran a thumb down Truth-Teller's black hilt, the silver runes on the dark scabbard shimmering in the light. "What about the human queens?"

"We continue to watch. *You* continue to watch."

"Vassa and Jurian are still with Graysen. Do we loop them in?"

A strange gathering, down in the human lands. With no queen ever having been appointed to the slice of territory at the base of Prythian, only a council of wealthy lords and merchants, Jurian had somehow stepped in to lead. Using Graysen's family estate as his seat of command.

And Vassa . . . She had stayed. Her *keeper* had granted her a reprieve from her curse—the enchantment that turned her into a firebird by day, woman again by night. And bound her to his lake deep in the continent.

I'd never seen such spell work. I'd sent my power over her, Helion too, hunting for any possible threads to unbind it. I found none. It was as if the curse was woven into her very blood.

But Vassa's freedom would end. Lucien had said as much months ago, and still visited her often enough that I knew nothing in that regard had improved. She would have to return to the lake, to the sorcerer-lord who kept her prisoner, sold to him by the very queens who had again gathered in their joint castle. Formerly Vassa's castle, too.

"Vassa knows that the Queens of the Realm will be a threat until they are dealt with," I said at last. Another tidbit that Lucien had told us. Well, Az and me at least. "But unless the queens step out of line, it's not for us to face. If we sweep in, even to stop them from triggering another war, we'll be seen as conquerors, not heroes. We need the humans in other territories to trust us, if we can ever hope to achieve lasting peace."

"Then perhaps Jurian and Vassa should deal with them. While Vassa is free to do so."

I'd contemplated it. Feyre and I had discussed it long into the night. Several times. "The humans must be given a chance to rule themselves. Decide for themselves. Even our allies."

"Send Lucien, then. As our human emissary."

I studied the tenseness in Azriel's shoulders, the shadows veiling half of him from the sunlight. "Lucien is away right now."

Az's brows rose. "Where?"

I winked at him. "You're my spymaster. Shouldn't you know?"

Az crossed his arms, face as elegant and cold as the legendary dagger at his side. "I don't make a point of looking after his movements."

"Why?"

Not a flicker of emotion. "He is Elain's mate."

I waited.

"It would be an invasion of her privacy to track him."

To know when and if Lucien sought her out. What they did together.

"You sure about that?" I asked quietly.

Azriel's Siphons guttered, the stones turning as dark and foreboding as the deepest sea. "Where did Lucien go."

I straightened at the pure order in the words. But I said, voice slipping into a drawl, "He went to the Spring Court. He'll be there for Solstice."

"Tamlin kicked him out the last time."

"He did. But he invited him for the holiday." Likely because Tamlin realized he'd be spending it alone in that manor. Or whatever was left of it.

I had no pity where that was concerned.

Not when I could still feel Feyre's undiluted terror as Tamlin tore through the study. As he locked her in that house.

Lucien had let him do it, too. But I'd made my peace with him. Or tried to.

With Tamlin, it was more complicated than that. More complicated than I let myself usually dwell on.

He was still in love with Feyre. I couldn't blame him for it. Even if it made me want to rip out his throat.

I shoved the thought away. "I'll discuss Vassa and Jurian with Lucien when he returns. See if he's up for another visit." I angled my head. "Do you think he can handle being around Graysen?"

Az's expressionless face was precisely the reason he'd never lost to us at cards. "Why should I be the judge of that?"

"You mean to tell me that you *weren't* bluffing when you said you didn't track Lucien's every movement?"

Nothing. Absolutely nothing on that face, on his scent. The shadows, whatever the hell they were, hid too well. Too much. Azriel only said coldly, "If Lucien kills Graysen, then good riddance."

I was inclined to agree. So was Feyre—and Nesta.

"I'm half tempted to give Nesta hunting rights for Solstice."

"You're getting her a gift?"

No. Sort of. "I'd think bankrolling her apartment and drinking was gift enough."

Az ran a hand through his dark hair. "Are we . . ." Unusual for

him to stumble with words. "Are we supposed to get the sisters presents?"

"No," I said, and meant it. Az seemed to loose a sigh of relief. Seemed to, since all but a breath of air passed from his lips. "I don't think Nesta gives a shit, and I don't think Elain expects to receive anything from us. I'd leave the sisters to exchange presents amongst themselves."

Az nodded distantly.

I drummed my fingers on the map, right over the Spring Court. "I can tell Lucien myself in a day or two. About going to Graysen's manor."

Azriel arched a brow. "You mean to visit the Spring Court?"

I wished I could say otherwise. But I instead told him what Eris had implied: that Tamlin either might not care to enforce his borders with the human realm or might be open to letting anyone through them. I doubted I'd get a decent night's rest until I found out for myself.

When I finished, Az picked at an invisible speck of dust on the leather scales of his gauntlet. The only sign of his annoyance. "I can go with you."

I shook my head. "It's better to do this on my own."

"Are you talking about seeing Lucien or Tamlin?"

"Both."

Lucien, I could stomach. Tamlin . . . Perhaps I didn't want any witnesses for what might be said. Or done.

"Will you ask Feyre to join you?" One look in Azriel's hazel eyes and I knew he was well aware of my reasons for going alone.

"I'll ask her in a few hours," I said, "but I doubt she will want

to come. And I doubt I will try my best to convince her to change her mind."

Peace. We had peace within our grasp. And yet there were debts left unpaid that I was not above righting.

Az nodded knowingly. He'd always understood me best—more than the others. Save my mate. Whether it was his gifts that allowed him to do so, or merely the fact that he and I were more similar than most realized, I'd never learned.

But Azriel knew a thing or two about old scores to settle. Imbalances to be righted.

So did most of my inner circle, I supposed.

"No word on Bryaxis, I take it." I peered toward the marble beneath my boots, as if I could see all the way to the library beneath this mountain and the now-empty lower levels that had once been occupied.

Az studied the floor as well. "Not a whisper. Or a scream, for that matter."

I chuckled. My brother had a sly, wicked sense of humor. I'd planned to hunt Bryaxis down for months now—to take Feyre and let her track down the entity that, for lack of a better explanation, seemed to be fear itself. But, as with so many of my plans for my mate, running this court and figuring out the world beyond it had gotten in the way.

"Do you want me to hunt it down?" An easy, unruffled question.

I waved a hand, my mating band catching in the morning light. That I hadn't heard from Feyre yet told me enough: still asleep. And as tempting as it was to wake her just to hear the sound of her voice, I had little desire to have my balls nailed to the wall for disrupting her sleep. "Let Bryaxis enjoy the Solstice as well," I said.

A rare smile curled Az's mouth. "Generous of you."

I inclined my head dramatically, the portrait of regal magnanimity, and dropped into my chair before propping my feet on the desk. "When do you head out for Rosehall?"

"The morning after Solstice," he supplied, turning toward the glittering sprawl of Velaris. He winced—slightly. "I still need to do some shopping before I go."

I offered my brother a crooked smile. "Buy her something from me, will you? And put it on my account this time."

I knew Az wouldn't, but he nodded all the same.

CHAPTER
8

Cassian

A storm was coming.

Right in time for Solstice. It wouldn't hit for another day or two, but Cassian could smell it on the wind. The others in the Windhaven camp could as well, the usual flurry of activity now a swift, efficient thrum. Houses and tents checked, stews and roasts being prepared, people departing or arriving earlier than expected to outrace it.

Cassian had given the girls the day off because of it. Had ordered all training and exercises, males included, to be postponed until after the storm. Limited patrols would still go out, only by those skilled and eager to test themselves against the sure-to-be-brutal winds and frigid temperatures. Even in a storm, enemies could strike.

If the storm was as great as he sensed it would be, this camp would be buried under snow for a good few days.

Which is why he wound up standing in the small craftsman center of the camp, beyond the tents and handful of permanent houses. Only a few shops occupied either side of the unpaved road, usually just a dirt track in warmer months. A general goods store, which had already posted a sold-out sign, two blacksmiths, a cobbler, a wood-carver, and a clothier.

The wooden building of the clothier was relatively new. At least by Illyrian standards—perhaps ten years old. Above the first-floor store seemed to be living quarters, lamps burning brightly within. And in the glass display window of the store: exactly what he'd come seeking.

A bell above the leaded-glass door tinkled as Cassian entered, tucking his wings in tight even with the broader-than-usual doorway. Warmth hit him, welcome and delicious, and he quickly shut the door behind him.

The slender young female behind the pine counter was already standing still. Watching him.

Cassian noticed the scars on her wings first. The careful, brutal scars down the center tendons.

Nausea roiled in his gut, even as he offered a smile and strode toward the polished counter. Clipped. She'd been clipped.

"I'm looking for Proteus," he said, meeting the female's brown eyes. Sharp and shrewd. Taken aback by his presence, but unafraid. Her dark hair was braided simply, offering a clear view of her tan skin and narrow, angular face. Not a face of beauty, but striking. Interesting.

Her eyes did not lower, not in the way Illyrian females had been ordered and trained to do. No, even with the clipping scars that proved traditional ways ran brutally deep in her family, she held his stare.

It reminded him of Nesta, that stare. Frank and unsettling.

"Proteus was my father," she said, untying her white apron to reveal a simple brown dress before she emerged from behind the counter. *Was.*

"I'm sorry," he said.

"He didn't come home from the war."

Cassian kept his chin from lowering. "I am even sorrier, then."

"Why should you be?" An unmoved, uninterested question. She extended a slender hand. "I'm Emerie. This is my shop now."

A line in the sand. And an unusual one. Cassian shook her hand, unsurprised to find her grip strong and unfaltering.

He'd known Proteus. Had been surprised when the male had joined the ranks during the war. Cassian knew he'd had one daughter and no sons. No close male relatives, either. With his death, the store would have gone to one of them. But for his daughter to step up, to insist this store was *hers*, and to keep running it . . . He surveyed the small, tidy space.

Glanced through the front window to the shop across the street, the sold-out sign there.

Stock filled Emerie's store. As if she'd just gotten a fresh shipment. Or no one had bothered to come in. Ever.

For Proteus to have owned and built this place, in a camp where the idea of shops was one that had only started in the past fifty or so years, meant he'd had a good deal of money. Enough perhaps for Emerie to coast on. But not forever.

"It certainly seems like it's your shop," he said at last, turning his attention back to her. Emerie had drifted a few feet away, her back straight, chin upraised.

He'd seen Nesta in that particular pose, too. He called it her *I Will Slay My Enemies* pose.

Cassian had named about two dozen poses for Nesta at this point.

Ranging from *I Will Eat Your Eyes for Breakfast* to *I Don't Want Cassian to Know I'm Reading Smut*. The latter was his particular favorite.

Suppressing his smile, Cassian gestured to the pretty piles of shearling-lined gloves and thick scarves that bedecked the window display. "I'll take every bit of winter gear you have."

Her dark brows rose toward her hairline. "Really?"

He fished a hand into the pocket of his leathers to pull out his money pouch and extended it to her. "That should cover it."

Emerie weighed the small leather pouch in her palm. "I don't need charity."

"Then take whatever the cost is for your gloves and boots and scarves and coats out of it and give the rest back to me."

She made no answer before chucking the pouch on the counter and bustling to the window display. Everything he asked for she gathered onto the counter in neat piles and stacks, even going into the back room behind the counter and emerging with more. Until there wasn't an empty bit of space on the polished counter, and only the sound of clinking coins filled the shop.

She wordlessly handed him back his pouch. He refrained from mentioning that she was one of the few Illyrians who'd ever accepted his money. Most had spat on it, or thrown it on the ground. Even after Rhys had become High Lord.

Emerie surveyed the piles of winter goods on the counter. "Do you want me to find some bags and boxes?"

He shook his head. "That won't be necessary."

Again, her dark brows rose.

Cassian reached into his money pouch and set three heavy coins onto the only sliver of empty space he could find on the counter. "For the delivery charges."

"To whom?" Emerie blurted.

"You live above the shop, don't you?" A terse nod. "Then I assume you know enough about this camp and who has plenty, and who has nothing. A storm is going to hit in a few days. I'd like you to distribute this amongst those who might feel its impact the hardest."

She blinked, and he saw her reassessment. Emerie studied the piled goods. "They—a lot of them don't like me," she said, more softly than he'd heard.

"They don't like me, either. You're in good company."

A reluctant curl of her lips at that. Not quite a smile. Certainly not with a male she didn't know.

"Consider it good advertising for this shop," he went on. "Tell them it was a gift from their High Lord."

"Why not you?"

He didn't want to answer that. Not today. "Better to leave me out of it."

Emerie took his measure for a moment, then nodded. "I'll make sure this has been delivered to those who need it most by sundown."

Cassian bowed his head in thanks and headed for the glass door. The door and windows on this building alone had likely cost more than most Illyrians could afford in years.

Proteus had been a wealthy man—a good businessman. And a decent warrior. To have risked this by going to war, he had to have possessed some shred of pride.

But the scars on Emerie's wings, proof that she'd never taste the wind again . . .

Half of him wished that Proteus were still alive. If only so he could kill the male himself.

Cassian reached for the brass handle, the metal cold against his palm.

"Lord Cassian."

He peered over a shoulder to where Emerie still stood behind the counter. He didn't bother to correct her, to say that he did not and would never accept using *lord* before his name. "Happy Solstice," she said tersely.

Cassian flashed her a smile. "You, too. Send word if you have any trouble with the deliveries."

Her narrow chin rose. "I'm sure I won't need to."

Fire in those words. Emerie would make the families take them, whether they wanted to or not.

He'd seen that fire before—and the steel. He half wondered what might happen if the two of them ever met. What might come of it.

Cassian shouldered his way out of the shop and into the freezing day, the bell tinkling in his wake. A herald of the storm to come.

Not just the storm that was barreling toward these mountains.

But perhaps one that had been brewing here for a long, long time.

CHAPTER
9

Feyre

I shouldn't have eaten dinner.

It was the thought tumbling through my head as I neared the studio Ressina occupied, darkness full overhead. As I saw the lights spilling into the frosted street, mixing with the glow from the lamps.

At this hour, three days before Solstice, it was packed with shoppers—not just residents of the quarter, but those from across the city and its countryside. So many High Fae and faeries, many of the latter kinds that I had never seen before. But all smiling, all seeming to shimmer with merriment and goodwill. It was impossible not to feel the thrum of that energy under my skin, even as nerves threatened to send me flying home, frigid wind or no.

I'd hauled a pack full of supplies down here, a canvas tucked under my arm, unsure whether they would be provided or if it would look rude to show up at Ressina's studio and appear to have *expected* to be given them. I'd walked from the town house, not wanting to winnow with so many things, and not wanting to risk losing the canvas to the tug of the bitter wind if I flew.

Staying warm aside, shielding against the wind while still *fly-ing* on the wind was something I'd yet to master, despite my now-occasional lessons with Rhys or Azriel, and with additional weight in my arms, plus the cold . . . I didn't know how the Illyrians did it, up in their mountains, where it was cold all year.

Perhaps I'd find out soon, if the grumblings and malcontent spread across the war-camps.

Not the time to think about it. My stomach was already uneasy enough.

I paused a house away from Ressina's studio, my palms sweating within my gloves.

I'd never painted with a group before. I rarely liked to share my paintings with anyone.

And this first time back in front of a canvas, unsure of what might come spilling out of me . . .

A tug on the bond.

Everything all right?

A casual, soft question, the cadence of Rhys's voice soothing the tremors along my nerves.

He'd told me where he planned to go tomorrow. What he planned to inquire about.

He'd asked me if I'd like to go with him.

I'd said no.

I might owe Tamlin my mate's life, I might have told Tamlin that I wished him peace and happiness, but I did not wish to see him. Speak with him. Deal with him. Not for a good long while. Perhaps forever.

Maybe it was because of that, because I'd felt worse after declining Rhys's invitation than I had when he'd asked, that I'd ventured out into the Rainbow tonight.

But now, faced with Ressina's communal studio, already hearing the laughter flitting out from where she and others had gathered for their weekly paint-in, my resolve sputtered out.

I don't know if I can do this.

Rhys was quiet for a moment. *Do you want me to come with you? To paint?*

I'd be an excellent nude model.

I smiled, not caring that I was by myself in the street with countless people streaming past me. My hood concealed most of my face, anyway. *You'll forgive me if I don't feel like sharing the glory that is you with anyone else.*

Perhaps I'll model for you later, then. A sensuous brush down the bond that had my blood heating. *It's been a while since we had paint involved.*

That cabin and kitchen table flashed into my mind, and my mouth went a bit dry. *Rogue.*

A chuckle. *If you want to go in, then go in. If you don't, then don't. It's your call.*

I frowned down at the canvas tucked under one arm, the box of paints cradled in the other. Frowned toward the studio thirty feet away, the shadows thick between me and that golden spill of light.

I know what I want to do.

⊹

No one noticed me winnow inside the boarded-up gallery and studio space down the street.

And with the boards over the windows, no one noticed the balls of faelight that I kindled and set to floating in the air on a gentle wind.

Of course, with the boards over empty windows, and no occupant for months, the main room was freezing. Cold enough that I set down my supplies and bounced on my toes as I surveyed the space.

It had probably been lovely before the attack: a massive window faced southward, letting in endless sunshine, and skylights—also boarded up—dotted the vaulted ceiling. The gallery in the front was perhaps thirty feet wide, fifty feet deep, with a counter against one wall halfway back, and a door to what had to be the studio space or storage in the rear. A quick examination told me I was half right: storage was in the back, but no natural light for painting. Only narrow windows above a row of cracked sinks, a few metal counters still stained with paint, and old cleaning supplies.

And paint. Not paint itself, but the *smell* of it.

I breathed in deep, feeling it settle into my bones, letting the quiet of the space settle, too.

The gallery up front had been her studio as well. Polina must have painted while she chatted with customers surveying the hung art whose outlines I could barely make out against the white walls.

The floors beneath them were gray stone, kernels of shattered glass still shining between the cracks.

I didn't want to do this first painting in front of others.

I could barely do it in front of myself. It was enough to drive away any guilt in regard to ignoring Ressina's offer to join her. I'd made her no promises.

So I summoned my flame to begin warming the space, setting little balls of it burning midair throughout the gallery. Lighting it further. Warming it back to life.

Then I went in search of a stool.

CHAPTER
10

Feyre

I painted and painted and painted.

My heart thundered the entire time, steady as a war-drum.

I painted until my back cramped and my stomach gurgled with demands for hot cocoa and dessert.

I'd known what needed to come out of me the moment I perched on the rickety stool I'd dusted off from the back.

I'd barely been able to hold the paintbrush steady enough to make the first few strokes. From fear, yes. I was honest enough with myself to admit that.

But also from the sheer unleashing of it, as if I were a racehorse freed from my pen, the image in my mind a dashing vision that I sprinted to keep up with.

But it began to emerge. Began to take form.

And in its wake, a sort of quiet followed, as if it were a layer of snow blanketing the earth. Clearing away what was beneath.

More cleansing, more soothing than any of the hours I'd spent rebuilding this city. Equally as fulfilling, yes, but the painting, the unleashing and facing it, was a release. A first stitch to close a wound.

The tower bells of Velaris sang twelve before I stopped.

Before I lowered my brush and stared at what I'd created.

Stared at what gazed back.

Me.

Or how I'd been in the Ouroboros, that beast of scale and claw and darkness; rage and joy and cold. All of me. What lurked beneath my skin.

I had not run from it. And I did not run from it now.

Yes—the first stitch to close a wound. That's how it felt.

With my brush dangling between my knees, with that beast forever on canvas, my body went a bit limp. Boneless.

I scanned the gallery, the street behind the boarded-up windows. No one had come to inquire about the lights in the hours I'd been here.

I stood at last, groaning as I stretched. I couldn't take it with me. Not when the painting had to dry, and the damp night air off the river and distant sea would be terrible for it.

I certainly wasn't going to bring it back to the town house for someone to find. Even Rhys.

But here . . . No one would know, should someone come in, who had painted it. I hadn't signed my name. Didn't want to.

If I left it here to dry overnight, if I came back tomorrow, there would certainly be some closet in the House of Wind where I might hide it afterward.

Tomorrow, then. I'd come back tomorrow to claim it.

CHAPTER
11

Rhysand

It was Spring, and yet it wasn't.

It was not the land I had once roamed in centuries past, or even visited almost a year ago.

The sun was mild, the day clear, distant dogwoods and lilacs still in eternal bloom.

Distant—because on the estate, nothing bloomed at all.

The pink roses that had once climbed the pale stone walls of the sweeping manor house were nothing but tangled webs of thorns. The fountains had gone dry, the hedges untrimmed and shapeless.

The house itself had looked better the day after Amarantha's cronies had trashed it.

Not for any visible signs of destruction, but for the general quiet. The lack of life.

Though the great oak doors were undeniably worse for wear. Deep, long claw marks had been slashed down them.

Standing on the top step of the marble staircase that led to those front doors, I surveyed the brutal gashes. My money was on Tamlin having inflicted them after Feyre had duped him and his court.

But Tamlin's temper had always been his downfall. Any bad day could have produced the gouge marks.

Perhaps today would produce more of them.

The smirk was easy to summon. So was the casual stance, a hand in the pocket of my black jacket, no wings or Illyrian leathers in sight, as I knocked on the ruined doors.

Silence.

Then—

Tamlin answered the door himself.

I wasn't sure what to remark on: the haggard male before me, or the dark house behind him.

An easy mark. Too easy of a mark, to mock the once-fine clothes desperate for a wash, the shaggy hair that needed a trim. The empty manor, not a servant in sight, no Solstice decorations to be found.

The green eyes that met mine weren't the ones I was accustomed to, either. Haunted and bleak. Not a spark.

It would be a matter of minutes to fillet him, body and soul. To finish what had undoubtedly started that day Feyre had called out silently at their wedding, and I had come.

But—peace. We had peace within our sights.

I could rip him apart after we attained it.

"Lucien claimed you would come," Tamlin said by way of greeting, voice as flat and lifeless as his eyes, a hand still braced on the door.

"Funny, I thought his mate was the seer."

Tamlin only stared at me, either ignoring or missing the humor. "What do you want."

No whisper of sound behind him. On any acre of this estate. Not even a note of birdsong. "I came to have a little chat." I offered him a half grin that I knew made him see red. "Can I trouble you for a cup of tea?"

⊹

The halls were dim, the embroidered curtains drawn.

A tomb.

This place was a tomb.

With each step toward what had once been the library, the dust and silence pressed in.

Tamlin didn't speak, didn't offer any explanations for the vacant house. For the rooms we passed, some of the carved doors cracked open enough for me to behold the destruction inside.

Shattered furniture, shredded paintings, cracked walls.

Lucien had not come here to make amends during Solstice, I realized as Tamlin opened the door to the dark library.

Lucien had come here out of pity. Mercy.

My sight adjusted to the darkness before Tamlin waved a hand, igniting the faelights in their glass bowls.

He hadn't destroyed this room yet. Had likely taken me to the one chamber in this house that had usable furniture.

I kept my mouth shut as we strode for a large desk in the center of the space, Tamlin claiming an ornate cushioned chair on one side of it. The only thing he had that was close to a throne these days.

I slid into the matching seat across from him, the pale wood groaning in protest. The set had likely been meant to accommodate tittering courtiers, not two full-grown warriors.

Quiet fell, as thick as the emptiness in this house.

"If you've come to gloat, you can spare yourself the effort."

I put a hand on my chest. "Why should I bother?"

No humor. "What did you want to talk about?"

I made a good show of surveying the books, the vaulted, painted ceiling. "Where's my dear friend Lucien?"

"Hunting for our dinner."

"No taste for such things these days?"

Tamlin's eyes remained dull. "He left before I was awake."

Hunting for dinner—because there were no servants here to make food. Or buy it.

I couldn't say I felt bad for him.

Only for Lucien, once again stuck with being his crony.

I crossed an ankle over a knee and leaned back in my chair. "What's this I hear about you not enforcing your borders?"

A beat of quiet. Then Tamlin gestured toward the door. "Do you see any sentries around to do it?"

Even they had abandoned him. Interesting. "Feyre did her work thoroughly, didn't she."

A flash of white teeth, a glimmer of light in his eyes. "With your coaching, I have no doubt."

I smiled. "Oh, no. That was all her. Clever, isn't she."

Tamlin gripped the curved arm of his chair. "I thought the High Lord of the Night Court couldn't be bothered to brag."

I didn't smile as I countered with, "I suppose you think I should be thanking you, for stepping up to assist in reviving me."

"I have no illusions that the day you thank me for anything, Rhysand, is the day the burning fires of hell go cold."

"Poetic."

A low snarl.

Too easy. It was far too easy to bait him, rile him. And though

I reminded myself of the wall, of the peace we needed, I said, "You saved my mate's life on several occasions. I will always be thankful for that."

I knew the words found their mark. *My mate.*

Low. It was a low blow. I had everything—*everything* I'd wished for, dreamed of, begged the stars to grant me.

He had nothing. Had been given everything and squandered it. He didn't deserve my pity, my sympathy.

No, Tamlin deserved what he'd brought upon himself, this husk of a life.

He deserved every empty room, every snarl of thorns, every meal he had to hunt for himself.

"Does she know you're here?"

"Oh, she certainly does." One look at Feyre's face yesterday when I'd invited her along had given me her answer before she'd voiced it: she had no interest in ever seeing the male across from me again.

"And," I went on, "she was as disturbed as I was to learn that your borders are not as enforced as we'd hoped."

"With the wall gone, I'd need an army to watch them."

"That can be arranged."

A soft snarl rumbled from Tamlin, and a hint of claws gleamed at his knuckles. "I'm not letting your ilk onto my lands."

"My *ilk*, as you call them, fought most of the war that *you* helped bring about. If you need patrols, I will supply the warriors."

"To protect humans from us?" A sneer.

My hands ached to wrap around his throat. Indeed, shadows curled at my fingertips, heralds of the talons lurking just beneath.

This house—I hated this house. Had hated it from the moment

I'd set foot in it that night, when Spring Court blood had flowed, payment for a debt that could never be repaid. Payment for two sets of wings, pinned in the study.

Tamlin had burned them long ago, Feyre had told me. It made no difference. He'd been there that day.

Had given his father and brothers the information on where my sister and mother would be waiting for me to meet them. And done nothing to help them as they were butchered.

I still saw their heads in those baskets, their faces still etched with fear and pain. And saw them again as I beheld the High Lord of Spring, both of us crowned in the same blood-soaked night.

"To protect humans from us, yes," I said, my voice going dangerously quiet. "To maintain the peace."

"What peace?" The claws slid back under his skin as he crossed his arms, less muscled than I'd last seen them on the battlefields. "Nothing is different. The wall is gone, that's all."

"We can make it different. Better. But only if we start off the right way."

"I'm not allowing one Night Court brute onto my lands."

His people despised him enough, it seemed.

And at that word—*brute*—I had enough. Dangerous territory. For me, at least. To let my own temper get the better of me. At least around him.

I rose from the chair, Tamlin not bothering to stand. "You brought every bit of this upon yourself," I said, my voice still soft. I didn't need to yell to convey my rage. I never had.

"You won," he spat, sitting forward. "You got your *mate*. Is that not enough?"

"No."

The word echoed through the library.

"You nearly destroyed her. In every way possible."

Tamlin bared his teeth. I bared mine back, temper be damned. Let some of my power rumble through the room, the house, the grounds.

"She survived it, though. Survived *you*. And you still felt the need to humiliate her, belittle her. If you meant to win her back, old friend, that wasn't the wisest route."

"Get out."

I wasn't finished. Not even close. "You deserve everything that has befallen you. You deserve this pathetic, empty house, your ravaged lands. I don't care if you offered that kernel of life to save me, I don't care if you still love my mate. I don't care that you saved her from Hybern, or a thousand enemies before that." The words poured out, cold and steady. "I hope you live the rest of your miserable life alone here. It's a far more satisfying end than slaughtering you." Feyre had once arrived at the same decision. I'd agreed with her then, still did, but now I truly understood.

Tamlin's green eyes went feral.

I braced for it, readied for it—*wanted* it. For him to explode out of that chair and launch himself at me, for his claws to start slashing.

My blood hammered in my veins, my power coiling inside me.

We could wreck this house in our fight. Bring it down to rubble. And then I'd turn the stones and wood into nothing but black dust.

But Tamlin only stared. And after a heartbeat, his eyes lowered to the desk. "Get out."

I blinked, the only sign of my surprise. "Not in the mood for a brawl, Tamlin?"

He didn't bother to look at me again. "Get out" was all he said.

A broken male.

Broken, from his own actions, his own choices.

It was not my concern. He did not deserve my pity.

But as I winnowed away, the dark wind ripping around me, a strange sort of hollowness took root in my stomach.

Tamlin didn't have shields around the house. None to prevent anyone from winnowing in, to guard against enemies appearing in his bedroom and slitting his throat.

It was almost as if he was waiting for someone to do it.

⊹

I found Feyre walking home from presumably doing some shopping, a few bags dangling from her gloved hands.

Her smile when I landed beside her, snow whipping around us, was like a fist to my heart.

It faded immediately, however, when she read my face.

Even in the middle of the busy city street, she put a hand to my cheek. "That bad?"

I nodded, leaning into her touch. The most I could manage.

She pressed a kiss to my mouth, her lips warm enough that I realized I'd gone cold.

"Walk home with me," she said, looping her arm through mine and pressing close.

I obeyed, taking the bags from her other hand. As the blocks passed and we crossed over the icy Sidra, then up the steep hills, I told her. Everything I'd said to Tamlin.

"Having heard you rip into Cassian, I'd say you were fairly mild," she observed when I'd finished.

I snorted. "Profanity wasn't necessary here."

She contemplated my words. "Did you go because you were concerned about the wall, or just because you wanted to say those things to him?"

"Both." I couldn't bring myself to lie to her about it. "And perhaps slaughter him."

Alarm flared in her eyes. "Where is this coming from?"

I didn't know. "I just . . ." Words failed me.

Her arm tightened around mine, and I turned to study her face. Open, understanding. "The things you said . . . they weren't wrong," she offered. No judgment, no anger.

Something still a bit hollow inside me filled slightly. "I should have been the bigger male."

"You're the bigger male most days. You're entitled to a slipup." She smiled broadly. Bright as the full moon, lovelier than any star.

I still had not gotten her a Solstice gift. And birthday present.

She angled her head at my frown, her braid slipping over a shoulder. I ran my hand along it, savoring the silken strands against my frozen fingers. "I'll meet you at home," I said, handing her the bags once more.

It was her turn to frown. "Where are you going?"

I kissed her cheek, breathing in her lilac-and-pear scent. "I have some errands that need tending to." And looking at her, walking beside her, did little to cool the rage that still roiled in me. Not when that beautiful smile made me want to winnow back to the Spring Court and punch my Illyrian blade through Tamlin's gut.

Bigger male indeed.

"Go paint my nude portrait," I told her, winking, and shot into the bitterly cold sky.

The sound of her laughter danced with me all the way to the Palace of Thread and Jewels.

✣

I surveyed the spread my preferred jeweler had laid out on black velvet atop the glass counter. In the lights of her cozy shop bordering the Palace, they flickered with an inner fire, beckoning.

Sapphires, emeralds, rubies . . . Feyre had them all. Well, in moderate amounts. Save for those cuffs of solid diamond I'd given her for Starfall.

She'd worn them only twice:

That night I had danced with her until dawn, barely daring to hope that she might be starting to return a fraction of what I felt for her.

And the night we'd returned to Velaris, after that final battle with Hybern. When she had worn *only* those cuffs.

I shook my head, and said to the slim, ethereal faerie behind the counter, "Beautiful as they are, Neve, I don't think milady wants jewels for Solstice."

A shrug that wasn't at all disappointed. I was a frequent enough customer that Neve knew she'd make a sale at some point.

She slid the tray beneath the counter and pulled out another, her night-veiled hands moving smoothly.

Not a wraith, but something similar, her tall, lean frame wrapped in permanent shadows, only her eyes—like glowing coals—visible. The rest tended to come in and out of view, as if the shadows parted to reveal a dark hand, a shoulder, a foot. Her people all master jewel smiths, dwelling in the deepest mountain mines in our court. Most of the heirlooms of our house had been Tartera-made, Feyre's cuffs and crowns included.

Neve waved a shadowed hand over the tray she'd laid out. "I had selected these earlier, if it's not too presumptuous, to consider for Lady Amren."

Indeed, these all *sang* Amren's name. Large stones, delicate settings. Mighty jewelry, for my mighty friend. Who had done so much for me, my mate—our people. The world.

I surveyed the three pieces. Sighed. "I'll take all of them."

Neve's eyes glowed like a living forge.

CHAPTER
12

Feyre

"What the hell is that?"

Cassian was grinning the next evening as he waved a hand toward the pile of pine boughs dumped on the ornate red rug in the center of the foyer. "Solstice decorations. Straight from the market."

Snow clung to his broad shoulders and dark hair, and his tan cheeks were flushed with cold. "You call that a decoration?"

He smirked. "A heap of pine in the middle of the floor is Night Court tradition."

I crossed my arms. "Funny."

"I'm serious." I glared, and he laughed. "It's for the mantels, the banister, and whatever else, smartass. Want to help?" He shrugged off his heavy coat, revealing a black jacket and shirt beneath, and hung it in the hall closet. I remained where I was and tapped my foot.

"What?" he said, brows rising. It was rare to see Cassian in anything but his Illyrian leathers, but the clothes, while not as fine as anything Rhys or Mor usually favored, suited him.

"Dumping a bunch of trees at my feet is really how you say hello these days? A little time in that Illyrian camp and you forget all your manners."

Cassian was on me in a second, hoisting me off the ground to twirl me until I was going to be sick. I beat at his chest, cursing at him.

Cassian set me down at last. "What'd you get me for Solstice?"

I smacked his arm. "A heaping pile of shut the hell up." He laughed again, and I winked at him. "Hot cocoa or wine?"

Cassian curved a wing around me, turning us toward the cellar door. "How many good bottles does little Rhysie have left?"

⊹

We drank two of them before Azriel arrived, took one look at our drunken attempts at decorating, and set about fixing it before anyone else could see the mess we'd made.

Lounging on a couch before the birch fire in the living room, we grinned like devils as the shadowsinger straightened the wreaths and garlands we'd chucked over things, swept up pine needles we'd scattered over the carpets, and generally shook his head at everything.

"Az, relax for a minute," Cassian drawled, waving a hand. "Have some wine. Cookies."

"Take off your coat," I added, pointing the bottle toward the shadowsinger, who hadn't even bothered to do so before fixing our mess.

Azriel straightened a sagging section of garland over the windowsill. "It's almost like you two *tried* to make it as ugly as possible."

Cassian clutched at his heart. "We take offense to that."

Azriel sighed at the ceiling.

"Poor Az," I said, pouring myself another glass. "Wine will make you feel better."

He glared at me, then the bottle, then Cassian . . . and finally stormed across the room, took the bottle from my hand, and chugged the rest. Cassian grinned with delight.

Mostly because Rhys drawled from the doorway, "Well, at least now I know who's drinking all my good wine. Want another one, Az?"

Azriel nearly spewed the wine into the fire, but made himself swallow and turn, red-faced, to Rhys. "I would like to explain—"

Rhys laughed, the rich sound bouncing off the carved oak moldings of the room. "Five centuries, and you think I don't know that if my wine's gone, Cassian's usually behind it?"

Cassian raised his glass in a salute.

Rhys surveyed the room and chuckled. "I can tell exactly which ones you two did, and which ones Azriel tried to fix before I got here." Azriel was indeed now rubbing his temple. Rhys lifted a brow at me. "I expected better from an artist."

I stuck out my tongue at him.

A heartbeat later, he said in my mind, *Save that tongue for later. I have ideas for it.*

My toes curled in their thick, high socks.

"It's cold as hell!" Mor called from the front hall, startling me from the warmth pooling in my core. "And who the hell let Cassian and Feyre decorate?"

Azriel choked on what I could have sworn was a laugh, his normally shadowed face lighting up as Mor bustled in, pink with cold and puffing air into her hands. She, however, scowled. "You two couldn't wait until I got here to break into the good wine?"

I grinned as Cassian said, "We were just getting started on Rhys's collection."

Rhys scratched his head. "It *is* there for anyone to drink, you know. Help yourself to whatever you want."

"Dangerous words, Rhysand," Amren warned, strutting through the door, nearly swallowed up by the enormous white fur coat she wore. Only her chin-length dark hair and solid silver eyes were visible above the collar. She looked—

"You look like an angry snowball," Cassian said.

I clamped my lips together to keep the laugh in. Laughing at Amren wasn't a wise move. Even now, with her powers mostly gone and permanently in a High Fae body.

The angry snowball narrowed her eyes at him. "Careful, boy. Wouldn't want to start a war you can't win." She unbuttoned the collar so we all heard her clearly as she purred, "Especially with Nesta Archeron coming for Solstice in two days."

I felt the ripple that went through them—between Cassian, and Mor, and Azriel. Felt the pure temper that rumbled from Cassian, all half-drunk merriness suddenly gone. He said in a low voice, "Shut it, Amren."

Mor was watching closely enough that it was hard not to stare. I glanced at Rhys instead, but a contemplative look had overtaken his face.

Amren merely grinned, those red lips spreading wide enough to show most of her white teeth as she stalked toward the front hall closet and said over a shoulder, "I'm going to enjoy seeing her shred into you. That's if she shows up sober."

And that was enough. Rhys seemed to arrive at the same idea, but before he could say something, I cut in, "Leave Nesta out of it, Amren."

Amren gave me what might have been considered an apologetic

glance. But she merely declared, shoving her enormous coat into the closet, "Varian's coming, so deal with it."

⊹

Elain was in the kitchen, helping Nuala and Cerridwen prepare the evening meal. Even with Solstice two nights away, everyone had descended upon the town house.

Except one.

"Any word from Nesta?" I said to my sister by way of greeting.

Elain straightened from the piping-hot loaves of bread she'd hauled from the oven, her hair half up, the apron over her rose-pink gown dusted with flour. She blinked, her large brown eyes clear. "No. I told her to join us tonight, and to let me know when she'd decided. I didn't hear back."

She waved a dishcloth over the bread to cool it slightly, then lifted a loaf to tap the bottom. A hollow sound thumped back, answer enough for her.

"Do you think it's worth fetching her?"

Elain slung the dishcloth over her slim shoulder, rolling her sleeves up to the elbow. Her skin had gained color these months—at least, before the cold weather had set in. Her face had filled in, too. "Are you asking me that as her sister, or as a seer?"

I kept my face calm, pleasant, and leaned against the worktable.

Elain had not mentioned any further visions. And we had not asked her to use her gifts. Whether they still existed, with the Cauldron's destruction and then re-forming, I didn't know. Didn't want to ask.

"You know Nesta best," I answered carefully. "I thought you'd like to weigh in."

"If Nesta doesn't want to be here tonight, then it's more trouble than it's worth to bring her in."

Elain's voice was colder than usual. I glanced at Nuala and Cerridwen, the latter giving me a shake of her head as if to say, *Not a good day for her.*

Like the rest of us, Elain's recovery was ongoing. She'd wept for hours the day I'd taken her to a wildflower-covered hill on the outskirts of the city—to the marble headstone I'd had erected there in honor of our father.

I'd turned his body to ashes after the King of Hybern had killed him, but he still deserved a resting place. For all he'd done in the end, he deserved the beautiful stone I'd had carved with his name. And Elain had deserved a place to visit with him, talk with him.

She went at least once a month.

Nesta had never been at all. Had ignored my invitation to come with us that first day. And every time afterward.

I took up a spot beside Elain, grabbing a knife from the other side of the table to begin cutting the bread. Down the hall, the sounds of my family echoed toward us, Mor's bright laughter ringing out above Cassian's rumble.

I waited until I had a stack of steaming slices before I said, "Nesta is still a part of this family."

"Is she?" Elain sawed deep into the next loaf. "She certainly doesn't act like it."

I hid my frown. "Did something happen when you saw her today?"

Elain didn't answer. She just kept slicing the bread.

So I continued as well. I didn't appreciate when other people pushed me to speak. I'd grant her that same courtesy, too.

In silence, we worked, then set about filling the platters with the food Nuala and Cerridwen signaled was ready, their shadows veiling them more than usual. To grant us some sense of privacy. I threw them a look of gratitude, but they both shook their heads. No thanks necessary. They'd spent more time with Elain than even I had. They understood her moods, what she sometimes needed.

It was only when Elain and I were hauling the first of the serving dishes down the hall toward the dining room that she spoke. "Nesta said she didn't want to come to Solstice."

"That's fine." Even though something in my chest twisted a bit.

"She said she didn't want to come to *anything*. Ever."

I paused, scanning the pain and fear now shining in Elain's eyes. "Did she say why?"

"No." Anger—there was anger in Elain's face, too. "She just said . . . She said that we have our lives, and she has hers."

To say that to me, fine. But to *Elain*?

I blew out a breath, my stomach gurgling at the platter of slow-roasted chicken I held between my hands, the scent of sage and lemon filling my nose. "I'll talk to her."

"Don't," Elain said flatly, starting once more into a walk, veils of steam drifting past her shoulders from the roasted rosemary potatoes in her hands, as if they were Azriel's shadows. "She won't listen."

Like hell she wouldn't.

"And you?" I made myself say. "Are you—all right?"

Elain looked over a shoulder at me as we entered the foyer, then turned left—to the dining room. In the sitting room across the way, all conversation halted at the smell of food. "Why wouldn't I be all right?" she asked, a smile lighting up her face.

I'd seen those smiles before. On my own damn face.

But the others came barreling in from the sitting room, Cassian kissing Elain's cheek in greeting before he nearly lifted her out of the way to get to the dining table. Amren came next, giving my sister a nod, her ruby necklace sparkling in the faelights speckled throughout the garlands in the hall. Then Mor, with a smacking kiss for either cheek. Then Rhys, shaking his head at Cassian, who began helping himself to the platters Nuala and Cerridwen winnowed in. As Elain lived here, my mate gave her only a smile of greeting before taking up his seat at Cassian's right.

Azriel emerged from the sitting room, a glass of wine in hand and wings tucked back to reveal his fine, yet simple black jacket and pants.

I felt, more than saw, my sister go still as he approached. Her throat bobbed.

"Are you just going to hold that chicken all night?" Cassian asked me from the table.

Scowling, I stomped toward him, plunking the platter onto the wooden surface. "I spat in it," I said sweetly.

"Makes it all the more delicious," Cassian crooned, smiling right back. Rhys snickered, drinking deeply from his wine.

But I strode to my seat—nestled between Amren and Mor—in time to see Elain say to Azriel, "Hello."

Az said nothing.

No, he just moved toward her.

Mor tensed beside me.

But Azriel only took Elain's heavy dish of potatoes from her hands, his voice soft as night as he said, "Sit. I'll take care of it."

Elain's hands remained in midair, as if the ghost of the dish remained between them. With a blink, she lowered them, and noticed her apron. "I—I'll be right back," she murmured, and hurried down the hall before I could explain that no one cared if she showed up to dinner covered in flour and that she should just *sit*.

Azriel set the potatoes in the center of the table, Cassian diving right in. Or he tried to.

One moment, his hand was spearing toward the serving spoon. The next, it was stopped, Azriel's scarred fingers wrapped around his wrist. "Wait," Azriel said, nothing but command in his voice.

Mor gaped wide enough that I was certain the half-chewed green beans in her mouth were going to tumble onto her plate. Amren just smirked over the rim of her wineglass.

Cassian gawked at him. "Wait for *what*? Gravy?"

Azriel didn't let go. "Wait until everyone is seated before eating."

"Pig," Mor supplied.

Cassian gave a pointed look to the plate of green beans, chicken, bread, *and* ham already half eaten on Mor's plate. But he relaxed his hand, leaning back in his chair. "I never knew you were a stickler for manners, Az."

Azriel only released Cassian's hand, and stared at his wineglass.

Elain swept in, apron gone and hair rebraided. "Please don't wait on my account," she said, taking the seat at the head of the table.

Cassian glared at Azriel. Az pointedly ignored him.

But Cassian waited until Elain had filled her plate before he took another scoop of anything. As did the others.

I met Rhys's stare across the table. *What was that about?*

Rhys sliced into his glazed ham in smooth, skilled strokes. *It had nothing to do with Cassian.*

Oh?

Rhys took a bite, gesturing with his knife for me to eat. *Let's just say it hit a little close to home.* At my beat of confusion, he added, *There are some scars when it comes to how his mother was treated. Many scars.*

His mother, who had been a servant—near-slave—when he was born. And afterward. *None of us bother to wait for everyone to sit, least of all Cassian.*

It can strike at odd times.

I did my best not to look toward the shadowsinger. *I see.*

Turning to Amren, I studied her plate. Small portions of everything. "Still getting used to it?"

Amren grunted, rolling around her roasted, honeyed carrots. "Blood tastes better."

Mor and Cassian choked.

"And it didn't take so much *time* to consume," Amren groused, lifting the teensiest scrap of roast chicken to her red-painted lips.

Small, slow meals for Amren. The first normal meal she'd eaten after returning—a bowl of lentil soup—had made her vomit for an hour. So it had been a gradual adjustment. She still couldn't dive into a meal the way the rest of us were prone to. Whether it was wholly physical or perhaps some sort of personal adjustment period, none of us knew.

"And then there are the other unpleasant results of eating," Amren went on, slicing her carrots into tiny slivers.

Azriel and Cassian swapped a glance, then both seemed to find their plates *very* interesting. Even as smiles tugged on their faces.

Elain asked, "What sort of results?"

"Don't answer that," Rhys said smoothly, pointing to Amren with his fork.

Amren hissed at him, her dark hair swaying like a curtain of liquid night, "Do you know what an inconvenience it is to need to find a place to relieve myself *everywhere I go*?"

A fizzing noise came from Cassian's side of the table, but I clamped my lips together. Mor gripped my knee beneath the table, her body shaking with the effort of keeping her laugh reined in.

Rhys drawled to Amren, "Shall we start building public toilets for you throughout Velaris, Amren?"

"I mean it, Rhysand," Amren snapped. I didn't dare meet Mor's stare. Or Cassian's. One look and I'd completely dissolve. Amren waved a hand down at herself. "I should have selected a male form. At least *you* can whip it out and go wherever you like without having to worry about spilling on—"

Cassian lost it. Then Mor. Then me. And even Az, chuckling faintly.

"You really don't know how to pee?" Mor roared. "After all this time?"

Amren seethed. "I've seen animals—"

"Tell me you know how a toilet works," Cassian burst out, slapping a broad hand on the table. "Tell me you know that much."

I clapped a hand over my mouth, as if it would push the laugh back in. Across the table, Rhys's eyes were brighter than stars, his mouth a quivering line as he tried and failed to remain serious.

"I know how to sit on a toilet," Amren growled.

Mor opened her mouth, laughter dancing on her face, but Elain asked, "Could you have done it? Decided to take a male form?"

The question cut through the laughter, an arrow fired between us.

Amren studied my sister, Elain's cheeks red from our unfiltered talk at the table. "Yes," she said simply. "Before, in my other form, I was neither. I simply *was*."

"Then why did you pick this body?" Elain asked, the faelight of the chandelier catching in the ripples of her golden-brown braid.

"I was more drawn to the female form," Amren answered simply. "I thought it was more symmetrical. It pleased me."

Mor frowned down at her own form, ogling her considerable assets. "True."

Cassian snickered.

Elain asked, "And once you were in this body, you couldn't change?"

Amren's eyes narrowed slightly. I straightened, glancing between them. Unusual, yes, for Elain to be so vocal, but she'd been improving. Most days, she was lucid—perhaps quiet and prone to melancholy, but aware.

Elain, to my surprise, held Amren's gaze.

Amren said after a moment, "Are you asking out of curiosity for my past, or your own future?"

The question left me too stunned to even reprimand Amren. The others, too.

Elain's brow furrowed before I could leap in. "What do you mean?"

"There's no going back to being human, girl," Amren said, perhaps a tad gently.

"Amren," I warned.

Elain's face reddened further, her back straightening. But she didn't bolt. "I don't know what you're talking about." I'd never heard Elain's voice so cold.

I glanced at the others. Rhys was frowning, Cassian and Mor were both grimacing, and Azriel . . . It was pity on his beautiful face. Pity and sorrow as he watched my sister.

Elain hadn't mentioned being Made, or the Cauldron, or

Graysen in months. I'd assumed that perhaps she was becoming accustomed to being High Fae, that she'd perhaps begun to let go of that mortal life.

"Amren, you have a spectacular gift for ruining dinner conversation," Rhys said, swirling his wine. "I wonder if you could make a career out of it."

His Second glared at him. But Rhys held her stare, silent warning in his face.

Thank you, I said down the bond. A warm caress echoed in answer.

"Pick on someone your own size," Cassian said to Amren, shoveling roast chicken into his mouth.

"I'd feel bad for the mice," Azriel muttered.

Mor and Cassian howled, earning a blush from Azriel and a grateful smile from Elain—and no shortage of scowling from Amren.

But something in me eased at that laughter, at the light that returned to Elain's eyes.

A light I wouldn't see dimmed further.

I need to go out after dinner, I said to Rhys as I dug into my meal again. *Care for a flight across the city?*

Nesta didn't open her door.

I knocked for perhaps a good two minutes, scowling at the dim wooden hallway of the ramshackle building that she'd chosen to live in, then sent a tether of magic through the apartment beyond.

Rhys had erected wards around the entire thing, and with our magic, our souls' bond, there was no resistance to the thread of power I unspooled through the door and into the apartment itself.

Nothing. No sign of life or——or worse beyond.

She wasn't at home.

I had a good idea of where she'd be.

Winnowing into the freezing street, I pinwheeled my arms to keep upright as my boots slid on the ice coating the stones.

Leaning against a lamppost, faelight gilding the talons atop his wings, Rhys chuckled. And didn't move an inch.

"Asshole," I muttered. "Most males would *help* their mates if they're about to break their heads on the ice."

He pushed off the lamppost and prowled toward me, every movement smooth and unhurried. Even now, I'd gladly spend hours just watching him.

"I have a feeling that if I *had* stepped in, you would have bitten my head off for being an overbearing mother hen, as you called me."

I grumbled an answer he chose not to hear.

"Not at home, then?"

I grumbled again.

"Well, that leaves precisely ten other places where she could be."

I grimaced.

Rhys asked, "Do you want me to look?"

Not physically, but use his power to find Nesta. I hadn't wanted him to do it earlier, since it felt like some sort of violation of privacy, but given how damned *cold* it was . . . "Fine."

Rhys wrapped his arms, then his wings around me, tucking me into his heat as he murmured onto my hair, "Hold on."

Darkness and wind tumbled around us, and I buried my face in his chest, breathing in the scent of him.

Then laughter and singing, music blaring, the tangy smell of stale ale, the bite of cold——

I groaned as I beheld where he'd winnowed us, where he'd detected my sister.

"There are wine rooms in this city," Rhys said, cringing. "There are concert halls. Fine restaurants. Pleasure clubs. And yet your sister . . ."

And yet my sister managed to find the seediest, most miserable taverns in Velaris. There weren't many. But she patronized all of them. And this one—the Wolf's Den—was by far the worst.

"Wait here," I said over the fiddles and drums spilling from the tavern as I pulled out of his embrace. Down the street, a few drunk revelers spotted us and fell silent. Felt Rhys's power, perhaps my own as well, and found somewhere else to be for a while.

I had no doubt the same would happen in the tavern, and had no doubt Nesta would resent us for ruining her night. At least I could slip inside mostly unnoticed. If both of us went in there, I knew my sister would see it as an attack.

So it would be me. Alone.

Rhys kissed my brow. "If someone propositions you, tell them we'll both be free in an hour."

"Och." I waved him off, banking my powers to a near-whisper within me.

He blew me a kiss.

I waved that away, too, and slipped through the tavern door.

CHAPTER
13

Feyre

My sister didn't have drinking companions. As far as I knew, she went out alone, and made them as the night progressed. And every now and then, one of them went home with her.

I hadn't asked. Wasn't even sure when the first time had been.

I also didn't dare ask Cassian if he knew. They had barely exchanged more than a few words since the war.

And as I entered the light and rolling music of the Wolf's Den and immediately spotted my sister seated with three males at a round table in the shadowed back, I could almost see the specter of that day against Hybern looming behind her.

Every ounce of weight that Elain had gained it seemed Nesta had lost. Her already proud, angular face had turned more so, her cheekbones sharp enough to slice. Her hair remained up in her usual braided coronet, she wore her preferred gray gown, and she was, as ever, immaculately clean despite the hovel she chose to occupy. Despite the reeking, hot tavern that had seen better years. Centuries.

A queen without a throne. That was what I'd call the painting that swept into my mind.

Nesta's eyes, the same blue-gray as my own, lifted the moment I shut the wooden door behind me. Nothing flickered across her face beyond vague disdain. The three High Fae males at her table were all fairly well dressed considering the place they patronized.

Likely wealthy young bucks out for the night.

I reined in my scowl as Rhys's voice filled my head. *Mind your own business.*

Your sister is handily beating them at cards, by the way.

Snoop.

You love it.

I pressed my lips together, sending a vulgar gesture down the bond as I approached my sister's table. Rhys's laughter rumbled against my shields in answer, like star-flecked thunder.

Nesta simply went back to staring at the fan of cards she held, her posture the epitome of glorious boredom. But her companions peered up at me when I stopped at the edge of their stained and scarred wooden table. Half-consumed glasses of amber liquid sweated with moisture, kept chilled through some magic of the tavern's.

The male across the table—a handsome, rakish-looking High Fae, with hair like spun gold—met my eyes.

His hand of cards slumped to the table as he bowed his head. The others followed suit.

Only my sister, still studying her cards, remained uninterested.

"My lady," said a thin, dark-haired male, throwing a wary glance toward my sister. "How may we be of assistance?"

Nesta didn't so much as look up as she adjusted one of her cards.

Fine.

I smiled sweetly at her companions. "I hate to interrupt your night out, gentlemen." Gentle*males*, I supposed. A holdover from my human life—one that the third male noted with a hint of a raised, thick brow. "But I would like a word with my sister."

The dismissal was clear enough.

As one, they rose, cards abandoned, and swiped up their drinks. "We'll get a refill," the golden-haired one declared.

I waited until they were at the bar, pointedly not gazing over their shoulders, before I slid into the rickety seat the dark-haired one had vacated.

Slowly, Nesta's eyes lifted toward mine.

I leaned back in the chair, wood groaning. "So which one was going home with you tonight?"

Nesta snapped her cards together, setting the stack facedown on the table. "I hadn't decided."

Icy, flat words. The perfect accompaniment to the expression on her face.

I simply waited.

Nesta waited, too.

Still as an animal. Still as death.

I'd once wondered if that was her power. Her curse, granted by the Cauldron.

Nothing I'd seen of it, glimpsed in those moments against Hybern, had seemed *like* death. Just brute power. But the Bone Carver had whispered of it. And I'd seen it, shining cold and bright in her eyes.

But not for months now.

Not that I'd seen much of her.

A minute passed. Then another.

Utter silence, save for the merry music from the four-piece band on the other side of the room.

I could wait. I'd wait here all damn night.

Nesta settled back in her chair, inclined to do the same.

My money's on your sister.

Quiet.

I'm getting cold out here.

Illyrian baby.

A dark chuckle, then the bond went silent again.

"Is that mate of yours going to stand in the cold all night?"

I blinked, wondering if she'd somehow sensed the thoughts between us. "Who says he's here?"

Nesta snorted. "Where one goes, the other follows."

I refrained from voicing all of the potential retorts that leaped onto my tongue.

Instead, I asked, "Elain invited you to dinner tonight. Why didn't you come?"

Nesta's smile was slow, sharp as a blade. "I wanted to hear the musicians play."

I cast a pointed look to the band. More skilled than the usual tavern set, but not a real excuse. "She wanted you there." *I wanted you there.*

Nesta shrugged. "She could have eaten with me here."

"You know Elain wouldn't feel comfortable in a place like this."

She arched a well-groomed brow. "A place like this? What sort of place is that?"

Indeed, some people were turning our way. High Lady—I was

High Lady. Insulting this place and the people in it wouldn't win me any supporters. "Elain is overwhelmed by crowds."

"She didn't used to be that way." Nesta swirled her glass of amber liquid. "She loved balls and parties."

The words hung unspoken. *But you and your court dragged us into this world. Took that joy away from her.*

"If you bothered to come by the house, you'd see that she's readjusting. But balls and parties are one thing. Elain never patronized taverns before this."

Nesta opened her mouth, no doubt to lead me down a path away from the reason I'd come here. So I cut in before she could. "That's beside the point."

Steel-cold eyes held mine. "Can you get to it, then? I'd like to return to my game."

I debated scattering the cards to the ale-slick ground. "Solstice is the day after tomorrow."

Nothing. Not a blink.

I interlaced my fingers and set them on the table between us. "What will it take to get you to come?"

"For Elain's sake or yours?"

"Both."

Another snort. Nesta surveyed the room, everyone carefully *not* watching us now. I knew without asking that Rhys had slid a sound barrier around us.

Finally, my sister looked back at me. "So you're bribing me, then?"

I didn't flinch. "I'm seeing if you're willing to be reasoned with. If there's a way to make it worth your while."

Nesta planted the tip of her pointer finger atop her stack of cards and fanned them out across the table. "It's not even our holi-day. We don't *have* holidays."

"Perhaps you should try it. You might enjoy yourself."

"As I told Elain: you have your lives, and I have mine."

Again, I cast a pointed glance to the tavern. "Why? Why this insistence on distancing yourself?"

She settled back in her seat, crossing her arms. "Why do I have to be a part of your merry little band?"

"You're my sister."

Again, that empty, cold look.

I waited.

"I'm not going to your party," she said.

If Elain hadn't been able to convince her, I certainly wouldn't succeed. I didn't know why I hadn't realized it before. Before wast-ing my time. But I tried—one last time. For Elain's sake. "Father would want you to—"

"Don't you finish that sentence."

Despite the sound shield around us, there was nothing to block the view of my sister baring her teeth. The view of her fingers curl-ing into invisible claws.

Nesta's nose crinkled with undiluted rage as she snarled, *"Leave."*

A scene. This was about to become a scene in the worst way.

So I rose, hiding my trembling hands by balling them into tight fists at my sides. "Please come," was all I said before turning back toward the door, the walk between her table and the exit feeling so much longer. All the staring faces I'd have to pass looming.

"My rent," Nesta said when I'd walked two steps.

I paused. "What about your rent?"

She swigged from her glass. "It's due next week. In case you forgot."

She was completely serious.

I said flatly, "Come to Solstice and I'll make sure it's delivered."

Nesta opened her mouth, but I turned again, staring down every gaping face that peered up at me as I passed.

I felt my sister's gaze piercing the space between my shoulder blades the entire walk to that front door. And the entire flight home.

CHAPTER
14

Rhysand

Even with workers seldom halting their repairs, the rebuilding was still years from being finished. Especially along the Sidra, where Hybern had hit hardest.

Little more than rubble remained of the once-great estates and homes along the southeastern bend of the river, their gardens overgrown and private boathouses half sunken in the gentle flow of the turquoise waters.

I'd grown up in these houses, attending the parties and feasts that lasted long into the night, spending bright summer days lazing on the sloping lawns, cheering the summer boat races on the Sidra. Their facades had been as familiar as any friend's face. They'd been built long before I was born. I'd expected them to last long after I was gone.

"You haven't heard from the families about when they'll be returning, have you?"

Mor's question floated to me above the crunch of pale stone beneath our feet as we ambled along the snow-dusted grounds of one such estate.

She'd found me after lunch—a rare, solitary meal these days. With Feyre and Elain out shopping in the city, when my cousin had appeared in the foyer of the town house, I hadn't hesitated to invite her for a walk.

It had been a long while since Mor and I had walked together.

I wasn't stupid enough to believe that though the war had ended, all wounds had been healed. Especially between Mor and me.

And I wasn't stupid enough to delude myself into thinking that I hadn't put off this walk for a while now—and so had she.

I'd seen her eyes go distant the other night at the Hewn City. Her silence after her initial snarled warning at her father had told me enough about where her mind had drifted.

Another casualty of this war: working with Keir and Eris had dimmed something in my cousin.

Oh, she hid it well. Save for when she was face-to-face with the two males who had—

I didn't let myself finish the thought, summon the memory. Even five centuries later, the rage threatened to swallow me until I'd left the Hewn City and Autumn Court in ruins.

But those were her deaths to claim. They always had been. I had never asked why she'd waited so long.

We'd quietly meandered through the city for half an hour now, going mostly unnoticed. A small blessing of Solstice: everyone was too busy with their own preparations to mark who strolled through the packed streets.

How we'd wound up here, I had no idea. But here we were, nothing but the fallen and cracked blocks of stone, winter-dry weeds, and gray sky for company.

"The families," I said at last, "are at their other estates." I knew them all, wealthy merchants and nobles who had defected from the

Hewn City long before the two halves of my realm had been offi-cially severed. "With no plans to return anytime soon." Perhaps for-ever. I'd heard from one of them, a matriarch of a merchant empire, that they were likely going to sell rather than face the ordeal of building from scratch.

Mor nodded absently, the chill wind whipping strands of her hair over her face as she paused in the middle of what had once been a formal garden sloping from the house to the icy river itself. "Keir is coming here soon, isn't he."

So rarely would she ever refer to him as her father. I didn't blame her. That male hadn't been her father for centuries. Long before that unforgivable day.

"He is."

I'd managed to keep Keir at bay since the war had ended—had prepared for him to inevitably decide that no matter the work I dumped in his lap, no matter how I might interrupt his little visits with Eris, he would visit this city.

Perhaps I had brought this upon myself, by enforcing the Hewn City's borders for so long. Perhaps their horrible traditions and nar-row minds had only grown worse while being contained. It was their territory, yes, but I'd given them nothing else. No wonder they were so curious about Velaris. Though Keir's desire to visit only stemmed from one need: to torment his daughter.

"When."

"Likely in the spring, if I'm guessing correctly."

Mor's throat bobbed, her face going cold in a way I so rarely wit-nessed. In a way I hated, if only because I was to blame for it.

I'd told myself it had been worth it. Keir's Darkbringers had been crucial in our victory. And he'd suffered losses because of it.

The male was a prick in every sense of the word, but he'd come through on his end.

I had little choice but to hold up my own.

Mor scanned me from head to toe. I'd opted for a black jacket crafted from heavier wool, and forgone wings entirely. Just because Cassian and Azriel had to suffer through having them be freezing all the time didn't mean I had to. I remained still, letting Mor arrive at her own conclusions. "I trust you," she said at last.

I bowed my head. "Thank you."

She waved a hand, launching into a walk again down the pale gravel paths of the garden. "But I still wish there had been another way."

"I do, too."

She twisted the ends of her thick red scarf before tucking them into her brown overcoat.

"If your father comes here," I offered, "I can make sure you're away." No matter that she had been the one to push for the minor confrontation with the Steward and Eris the other night.

She scowled. "He'll see it for what it is: hiding. I won't give him that satisfaction."

I knew better than to ask if she thought her mother would come along. We didn't discuss Mor's mother. Ever.

"Whatever you decide, I'll support you."

"I know that." She paused between two low-lying boxwoods and watched the icy river beyond.

"And you know that Az and Cassian are going to be monitoring them like hawks for the entire visit. They've been planning the security protocols for months now."

"They have?"

I nodded gravely.

Mor blew out a breath. "I wish we were still able to threaten to unleash Amren on the entire Hewn City."

I snorted, gazing across the river to the quarter of the city just barely visible over the rise of a hill. "Half of me wonders if Amren wishes the same."

"I assume you're getting her a *very* good present."

"Neve was practically skipping with glee when I left the shop."

A small laugh. "What did you get Feyre?"

I slid my hands into my pockets. "This and that."

"So, nothing."

I dragged a hand through my hair. "Nothing. Any ideas?"

"She's your mate. Shouldn't this sort of thing be instinctual?"

"She's impossible to shop for."

Mor gave me a wry look. "Pathetic."

I nudged her with an elbow. "What did *you* get her?"

"You'll have to wait until Solstice evening to see."

I rolled my eyes. In the centuries I'd known her, Mor's present-buying abilities had never improved. I had a drawer full of downright hideous cuff links that I'd never worn, each gaudier than the next. I was lucky, though: Cassian had a trunk crammed with silk shirts of varying colors of the rainbow. Some even had ruffles on them.

I could only imagine the horrors in store for my mate.

Thin sheets of ice lazily drifted down the Sidra. I didn't dare ask Mor about Azriel—what she'd gotten him, what she planned to *do* with him. I had little interest in being chucked right into that icy river.

"I'm going to need you, Mor," I said quietly.

The amusement in Mor's eyes sharpened to alertness. A predator. There was a reason she'd held her own in battle, and could hold her own against any Illyrian. My brothers and I had overseen much of the training ourselves, but she'd spent years traveling to other lands, other territories, to learn what they knew.

Which was precisely why I said, "Not with Keir and the Hewn City, not with holding the peace long enough for things to stabilize."

She crossed her arms, waiting.

"Az can infiltrate most courts, most lands. But I might need you to win those lands over." Because the pieces that were now strewn on the table . . . "Treaty negotiations are dragging on too long."

"They're not happening at all."

Truth. With the rebuilding, too many tentative allies had claimed they were busy and would reconvene in the spring to discuss the new terms.

"You wouldn't need to be gone for months. Just visits here and there. Casual."

"Casual, but make the kingdoms and territories realize that if they push too far or enter into human lands, we'll obliterate them?"

I huffed a laugh. "Something like that. Az has lists of the kingdoms most likely to cross the line."

"If I'm flitting about the continent, who will deal with the Court of Nightmares?"

"I will."

Her brown eyes narrowed. "You're not doing this because you think I can't handle Keir, are you?"

Careful, careful territory. "No," I said, and wasn't lying. "I think you can. I know you can. But your talents are better wielded else-where for now. Keir wants to build ties to the Autumn Court—let him. Whatever he and Eris are scheming up, they know we're watching, and know how stupid it would be for either of them to push us. One word to Beron, and Eris's head will roll."

Tempting. So damn tempting to tell the High Lord of Autumn that his eldest son coveted his throne—and was willing to take it by force. But I'd made a bargain with Eris, too. Perhaps a fool's bar-gain, but only time would tell in that regard.

Mor fiddled with her scarf. "I'm not afraid of them."

"I know you're not."

"I just—being near them, *together* . . ." She shoved her hands into her pockets. "It's probably what it feels like for you to be around Tamlin."

"If it's any consolation, cousin, I behaved rather poorly the other day."

"Is he dead?"

"No."

"Then I'd say you controlled yourself admirably."

I laughed. "Bloodthirsty of you, Mor."

She shrugged, again watching the river. "He deserves it."

He did indeed.

She glanced sidelong at me. "When would I need to leave?"

"Not for another few weeks, maybe a month."

She nodded, and fell quiet. I debated asking her if she wished to know *where* Azriel and I thought she might go first, but her silence said enough. She'd go anywhere.

Too long. She'd been cooped up within the borders of this court for too long. The war barely counted. And it wouldn't happen in a month, or perhaps a few years, but I could see it: the invisible noose tightening around her neck with every day spent here.

"Take a few days to think about it," I offered.

She whipped her head toward me, golden hair catching in the light. "You said you needed me. It didn't seem like there was much room for choice."

"You always have a choice. If you don't want to go, then it's fine."

"And who would do it instead? Amren?" A knowing look.

I laughed again. "Certainly not Amren. Not if we want peace." I added, "Just—do me a favor and take some time to think about it before you say yes. Consider it an offer, not an order."

She fell silent once more. Together, we watched the ice floes drift down the Sidra, toward the distant, wild sea. "Does he win if I go?" A quiet, tentative question.

"You have to decide that for yourself."

Mor turned toward the ruined house and grounds behind us. Staring not at them, I realized, but eastward.

Toward the continent and the lands within. As if wondering what might be waiting there.

CHAPTER
15

Feyre

I had yet to find or even come up with a vague idea for what to give Rhysand for Solstice.

Mercifully, Elain quietly approached me at breakfast, Cassian still passed out on the couch in the sitting room across the foyer and no sign of Azriel where he'd fallen asleep on the couch across from him, both too lazy—and perhaps a little drunk, after all the wine we'd had last night—to make the trek up to the tiny spare bedroom they'd be sharing during Solstice. Mor had taken my old bedroom, not minding the clutter I'd added, and Amren had gone back to her own apartment when we'd finally drifted to sleep in the early hours of the morning. Both my mate and Mor were still sleeping, and I'd been content to let them continue doing so. They'd earned that rest. We all had.

But Elain, it seemed, was as sleepless as me, especially after my stinging talk with Nesta that even the wine I'd returned home to drink couldn't dull, and she wanted to see if I was game for a walk about the city, providing me with the perfect excuse to head out for more shopping.

Decadent—it felt decadent, and selfish, to shop, even if it was for people I loved. There were so many in this city and beyond it who had next to nothing, and every additional, unnecessary moment I spent peering into window displays and running my fingers over various goods grated against my nerves.

"I know it's not easy for you," Elain observed as we drifted through a weaver's shop, admiring the fine tapestries, rugs, and blankets she'd crafted into images of various Night Court scenes: Velaris under the glow of Starfall; the rocky, untamed shores of the northern isles; the stelae of the temples of Cesere; the insignia of this court, the three stars crowning a mountain peak.

I turned from a wall covering depicting that very image. "What's not easy?"

We kept our voices to a near-murmur in the quiet, warm space, more out of respect to the other browsers admiring the work.

Elain's brown eyes roved over the Night Court insignia. "Buying things without a dire need to do so."

In the back of the vaulted, wood-paneled shop, a loom thrummed and clicked as the dark-haired artist who made the pieces continued her work, pausing only to answer questions from customers.

So different. This space was so different from the cottage of horrors that had belonged to the Weaver in the Wood. To Stryga.

"We have everything we need," I admitted to Elain. "Buying presents feels excessive."

"It's their tradition, though," Elain countered, her face still flushed with the cold. "One that they fought and died to protect in the war. Perhaps that's the better way to think of it, rather than feeling guilty. To remember that this day means something to them. All of them, regardless of who has more, who has less, and in celebrating the traditions, even through the presents, we honor those who fought for its very existence, for the peace this city now has."

For a moment, I just stared at my sister, the wisdom she'd spoken. Not a whisper of those oracular abilities. Just clear eyes and an open expression. "You're right," I said, taking in the insignia rising before me.

The tapestry had been woven from fabric so black it seemed to devour the light, so black it almost strained the eye. The insignia, however, had been rendered in silver thread—no, not silver. A sort of iridescent thread that shifted with sparks of color. Like woven starlight.

"You're thinking of getting it?" Elain asked. She hadn't bought anything in the hour we'd already been out, but she'd stopped often enough to contemplate. A gift for Nesta, she'd said. She was looking for a gift for our sister, regardless of whether Nesta deigned to join us tomorrow.

But Elain had seemed more than content to simply watch the humming city, to take in the sparkling strands of faelights strung between buildings and over the squares, to sample any tidbit of food offered by an eager vendor, to listen to minstrels busking by the now-silent fountains.

As if my sister, too, had merely been looking for an excuse to get out of the house today.

"I don't know *who* I'd get it for," I admitted, extending a finger toward the black fabric of the tapestry. The moment my nail touched the velvet-soft surface, it seemed to vanish. As if the material truly did gobble up all color, all light. "But . . ." I looked toward the weaver at the other end of the space, another piece half-formed on her loom. Leaving my thought unfinished, I strode for her.

The weaver was High Fae, full-figured and pale-skinned. A sheet of black hair had been braided back from her face, the length of the plait dropping over the shoulder of her thick, red sweater. Practical brown pants and shearling-lined boots completed her attire. Simple, comfortable clothes. What I might wear while painting. Or doing anything.

What I was wearing beneath my heavy blue overcoat, to be honest.

The weaver halted her work, deft fingers stilling, and lifted her head. "How can I help you?"

Despite her pretty smile, her gray eyes were . . . quiet. There was no way of explaining it. Quiet, and a little distant. The smile tried to offset it, but failed to mask the heaviness lingering within.

"I wanted to know about the tapestry with the insignia," I said. "The black fabric—what is it?"

"I get asked that at least once an hour," the weaver said, her smile remaining yet no humor lighting her eyes.

I cringed a bit. "Sorry to add to that." Elain drifted to my side, a fuzzy pink blanket in one hand, a purple blanket in the other.

The weaver waved off my apology. "It's an unusual fabric. Questions are expected." She smoothed a hand over the wooden frame of her loom. "I call it Void. It absorbs the light. Creates a complete lack of color."

"You made it?" Elain asked, now staring over her shoulder toward the tapestry.

A solemn nod. "A newer experiment of mine. To see how darkness might be made, woven. To see if I could take it farther, deeper than any weaver has before."

Having been in a void myself, the fabric she'd woven came unnervingly close. "Why?"

Her gray eyes shifted toward me again. "My husband didn't return from the war."

The frank, open words clanged through me.

It was an effort to hold her gaze as she continued, "I began trying to create Void the day after I learned he'd fallen."

Rhys hadn't asked anyone in this city to join his armies, though. Had deliberately made it a choice. At the confusion on my face, the weaver added softly, "He thought it was right. To help fight. He left with several others who felt the same, and joined up with a Summer Court legion they found on their way south. He died in the battle for Adriata."

"I'm sorry," I said softly. Elain echoed the words, her voice gentle.

The weaver only stared toward the tapestry. "I thought we'd have a thousand more years together." She began to coax the loom back into movement. "In the three hundred years we were wed, we never had the chance to have children." Her fingers moved beautifully, unfaltering despite her words. "I don't even have a piece of him in that way. He's gone, and I am not. Void was born of that feeling."

I didn't know what to say as her words settled in. As she continued working.

It could have been me.

It could have been Rhys.

That extraordinary fabric, created and woven in grief that I had briefly touched and never wished to know again, contained a loss I could not imagine recovering from.

"I keep hoping that every time I tell someone who asks about Void, it will get easier," the weaver said. If people asked about it as frequently as she'd claimed . . . I couldn't have endured it.

"Why not take it down?" Elain asked, sympathy written all over her face.

"Because I do not want to keep it." The shuttle swept across the loom, flying with a life of its own.

Despite her poise, her calm, I could almost feel her agony radiating into the room. A few touches of my daemati gifts and I might ease that grief, make the pain less. I'd never done so for anyone, but . . .

But I could not. Would not. It would be a violation, even if I made it with good intentions.

And her loss, her unending sorrow—she had created something from it. Something extraordinary. I couldn't take that away from her. Even if she asked me to.

"The silver thread," Elain asked. "What is that called?"

The weaver paused the loom again, the colorful strings vibrating. She held my sister's gaze. No attempt at a smile this time. "I call it Hope."

My throat became unbearably tight, my eyes stinging enough that I had to turn away, to walk back toward that extraordinary tapestry.

The weaver explained to my sister, "I made it after I mastered Void."

I stared and stared at the black fabric that was like peering into a pit of hell. And then stared at the iridescent, living silver thread that cut through it, bright despite the darkness that devoured all other light and color.

It could have been me. And Rhys. Had very nearly gone that way.

Yet he had lived, and the weaver's husband had not. *We* had lived, and their story had ended. She did not have a piece of him left. At least, not in the way she wished.

I was lucky—so tremendously *lucky* to even be complaining about shopping for my mate. That moment when he had died had been the worst of my life, would likely remain so, but we had survived it. These months, the *what-if* had haunted me. All of the *what-ifs* that we'd so narrowly escaped.

And this holiday tomorrow, this chance to celebrate being together, living . . .

The impossible depth of blackness before me, the unlikely defiance of Hope shining through it, whispered the truth before I knew it. Before I knew what I wanted to give Rhys.

The weaver's husband had not come home. But mine had.

"Feyre?"

Elain was again at my side. I hadn't heard her steps. Hadn't heard any sound for moments.

The gallery had emptied out, I realized. But I didn't care, not as I again approached the weaver, who had stopped once more. At the mention of my name.

The weaver's eyes were slightly wide as she bowed her head. "My lady."

I ignored the words. "How." I gestured to the loom, the half-finished piece taking form on its frame, the art on the walls. "How do you keep creating, despite what you lost?"

Whether she noted the crack in my voice, she didn't let on. The weaver only said, her sad, sorrowful gaze meeting mine, "I have to."

The simple words hit me like a blow.

The weaver went on, "I *have* to create, or it was all for nothing. I *have* to create, or I will crumple up with despair and never leave my bed. I *have* to create because I have no other way of voicing *this*."

Her hand rested on her heart, and my eyes burned. "It is hard," the weaver said, her stare never leaving mine, "and it hurts, but if I were to stop, if I were to let this loom or the spindle go silent . . ." She broke my gaze at last to look to her tapestry. "Then there would be no Hope shining in the Void."

My mouth trembled, and the weaver reached over to squeeze my hand, her callused fingers warm against mine.

I had no words to offer her, nothing to convey what surged in my chest. Nothing other than, "I would like to buy that tapestry."

⁜

The tapestry was a gift for no one but myself, and would be delivered to the town house later that afternoon.

Elain and I browsed various stores for another hour before I left my sister to do her own shopping at the Palace of Thread and Jewels.

I winnowed right into the abandoned studio in the Rainbow.

I needed to paint. Needed to get out what I'd seen, felt in the weaver's gallery.

I wound up staying for three hours.

Some paintings were quick, swift renderings. Some I began plotting out with pencil and paper, mulling over the canvas needed, the paint I'd like to use.

I painted through the grief that lingered at the weaver's story, painted *for* her loss. I painted all that rose within me, letting the past bleed onto the canvas, a blessed relief with each stroke of my brush.

It was little surprise I was caught.

I barely had time to leap off my stool before the front door opened and Ressina entered, a mop and bucket in her green hands. I certainly didn't have enough time to hide all the paintings and supplies.

Ressina, to her credit, only smiled as she stopped short. "I suspected you'd be in here. I saw the lights the other night and thought it might be you."

My heart pounded through my body, my face as warm as a forge, but I managed to offer a close-lipped smile. "Sorry."

The faerie gracefully crossed the room, even with the cleaning supplies in hand. "No need to apologize. I was just headed in to do some cleaning up."

She dumped the mop and bucket against one of the empty white walls with a faint thud.

"Why?" I laid my paintbrush atop the palette I'd placed on a stool beside mine.

Ressina set her hands on her narrow hips and surveyed the place.

By some mercy or lack of interest, she didn't look too long at my paintings. "Polina's family hasn't discussed whether they're selling, but I figured she, at least, wouldn't want the place to be a mess."

I bit my lip, nodding awkwardly as I lingered by the mess I'd added. "Sorry I . . . I didn't come by your studio the other night."

Ressina shrugged. "Again, no need to apologize."

So rarely did anyone outside the Inner Circle speak to me with such casualness. Even the weaver had become more formal after I'd offered to buy her tapestry.

"I'm just glad someone's using this place. That *you* are using it," Ressina added. "I think Polina would have liked you."

Silence fell when I didn't answer. When I began scooping up supplies. "I'll get out of your way." I moved to set down a still-drying painting against the wall. A portrait I'd been thinking about for some time now. I sent it to that pocket between realms, along with all the others I'd been working on.

I bent to pick up my pack of supplies.

"You could leave those."

I paused, a hand looped around the leather strap. "It's not my space."

Ressina leaned against the wall beside her mop and bucket. "Perhaps you could talk to Polina's family about that. They're motivated sellers."

I straightened, taking the supply pack with me. "Perhaps," I hedged, sending the rest of the supplies and paintings tumbling into that pocket realm, not caring if they crashed into each other as I headed for the door.

"They live out on a farm in Dunmere, by the sea. In case you're ever interested."

Not likely. "Thanks."

I could practically hear her smile as I reached the front door. "Happy Solstice."

"You, too," I threw over my shoulder before I vanished onto the street.

And slammed right into the hard, warm chest of my mate.

I rebounded off Rhys with a curse, scowling at his laugh as he gripped my arms to steady me against the icy street. "Going somewhere?"

I frowned at him, but linked my arm through his and launched into a brisk walk. "What are you doing here?"

"Why are you running out of an abandoned gallery as if you've stolen something?"

"I was not *running*." I pinched his arm, earning another deep, husky laugh.

"Walking suspiciously quickly, then."

I didn't answer until we'd reached the avenue that sloped down to the river. Thin crusts of ice drifted along the turquoise waters. Beneath them, I could feel the current still flowing past—not as strongly as I did in warmer months, though. As if the Sidra had fallen into a twilight slumber for the winter.

"That's where I've been painting," I said at last as we halted at the railed walkway beside the river. A damp, cold wind brushed past, ruffling my hair. Rhys tucked a strand of it behind my ear. "I went back today—and was interrupted by an artist, Ressina. But the studio belonged to a faerie who didn't survive the attack this spring. Ressina was cleaning up the space on her behalf. Polina's behalf, in case Polina's family wants to sell it."

"We can buy you a studio space if you need somewhere to paint by yourself," he offered, the thin sunlight gilding his hair. No sign of his wings.

"No—no, it's not being alone so much as . . . the right space to do it. The right *feel* to it." I shook my head. "I don't know. The painting helps. Helps me, I mean." I blew out a breath and surveyed him, the face dearer to me than anything in the world, the weaver's words echoing through me.

She had lost her husband. I had not. And yet she still wove, still created. I cupped Rhys's cheek, and he leaned into the touch as I quietly asked, "Do you think it's stupid to wonder if painting might help others, too? Not *my* painting, I mean. But teaching others to paint. Letting them paint. People who might struggle the same way I do."

His eyes softened. "I don't think that's stupid at all."

I traced my thumb over his cheekbone, savoring every inch of contact. "It makes me feel better—perhaps it would do the same for others."

He remained quiet, offering me that companionship that demanded nothing, asked nothing as I kept stroking his face. We had been mated for less than a year. If things had not gone well during that final battle, how many regrets would have consumed me? I knew—knew which ones would have hit the hardest, struck the deepest. Knew which ones were in my power to change.

I lowered my hand from his face at last. "Do you think anyone would come? If such a space, such a thing, were available?"

Rhys considered, scanning my eyes before kissing my temple, his mouth warm against my chilled face. "You'll have to see, I suppose."

⊹

I found Amren in her loft an hour later. Rhys had another meeting to attend with Cassian and their Illyrian commanders out at Devlon's war-camp, and had walked me to the door of her building before winnowing.

My nose crinkled as I entered Amren's toasty apartment. "It smells . . . interesting in here."

Amren, seated at the long worktable in the center of the space, gave me a slashing grin before gesturing to the four-poster bed.

Rumpled sheets and askew pillows said enough about what scents I was detecting.

"You could open a window," I said, waving to the wall of them at the other end of the apartment.

"It's cold out," was all she said, going back to—

"A jigsaw puzzle?"

Amren fitted a tiny piece into the section she'd been working on. "Am I supposed to be doing something else during my Solstice holiday?"

I didn't dare answer that as I shrugged off my overcoat and scarf. Amren kept the fire in the hearth near-sweltering. Either for herself, or her Summer Court companion, no sign of whom could I detect. "Where's Varian?"

"Out buying more presents for me."

"More?"

A smaller smile this time, her red mouth quirking to the side as she fitted another piece into her puzzle. "He decided the ones he brought from the Summer Court were not enough."

I didn't want to get into that comment, either.

I took a seat across from her at the long, dark wood table, examining the half-finished puzzle of what seemed to be some sort of autumnal pastoral. "A new hobby of yours?"

"Without that odious Book to decipher, I've found I miss such things." Another piece snapped into place. "This is my fifth this week."

"We're only three days into the week."

"They don't make them hard enough for me."

"How many pieces is this one?"

"Five thousand."

"Show-off."

Amren tutted to herself, then straightened in her chair, rubbing her back and wincing. "Good for the mind, but bad for the posture."

"Good thing you have Varian to exercise with."

Amren laughed, the sound like a crow's caw. "Good thing indeed." Those silver eyes, still uncanny, still limned with some trace of power, scanned me. "You didn't come here to keep me company, I suppose."

I leaned back in the rickety old chair. None at the table matched. Indeed, each seemed from a different decade. Century. "No, I didn't."

The High Lord's Second waved a hand tipped in long red nails and stooped over her puzzle again. "Proceed."

I took a steadying breath. "It's about Nesta."

"I suspected as much."

"Have you spoken to her?"

"She comes here every few days."

"Really?"

Amren tried and failed to fit a piece into her puzzle, her eyes darting over the color-sorted pieces around her. "Is it so hard to believe?"

"She doesn't come to the town house. Or the House of Wind."

"No one likes going to the House of Wind."

I reached for a piece and Amren clicked her tongue in warning. I set my hand back on my lap.

"I was hoping you might have some insight into what she's going through."

Amren didn't reply for a while, scanning the pieces laid out instead. I was about to repeat myself when she said, "I like your sister."

One of the few.

Amren lifted her eyes to me, as if I'd said the words aloud. "I like her because so few do. I like her because she is not easy to be around, or to understand."

"But?"

"But nothing," Amren said, returning to the puzzle. "Because I like her, I am not inclined to gossip about her current state."

"It's not gossip. I'm concerned." We all were. "She is starting down a path that—"

"I will not betray her confidence."

"She's talked to you?" Too many emotions cascaded through me at that. Relief that Nesta had talked to anyone, confusion that it had been *Amren*, and perhaps even some jealousy that my sister had not turned to me—or Elain.

"No," Amren said. "But I know she would not like me to be musing over her *path* with anyone. With you."

"But—"

"Give her time. Give her space. Give her the opportunity to sort through this on her own."

"It's been months."

"She's an immortal. Months are inconsequential."

I clenched my jaw. "She refuses to come home for Solstice. Elain will be heartbroken if she doesn't—"

"Elain, or you?"

Those silver eyes pinned me to the spot.

"Both," I said through my teeth.

Again, Amren sifted through her pieces. "Elain has her own problems to focus on."

"Such as?"

Amren just gave me a Look. I ignored it.

"If Nesta deigns to visit you," I said, the ancient chair groaning as I pushed it back and rose, grabbing my coat and scarf from the bench by the door, "tell her that it would mean a great deal if she came on Solstice."

Amren didn't bother to look up from her puzzle. "I will make no promises, girl."

It was the best I could hope for.

CHAPTER
16

Rhysand

That afternoon, Cassian dumped his leather bag on the narrow bed against the wall of the fourth bedroom in the town house, the contents rattling.

"You brought weapons to Solstice?" I asked, leaning against the door frame.

Azriel, setting his own bag on the bed opposite Cassian's, threw our brother a vague look of alarm. After passing out on the sitting room couches last night, and a likely uncomfortable sleep, they'd finally bothered to settle into the bedroom designated for them.

Cassian shrugged, plopping onto the bed, which was better suited for a child than an Illyrian warrior. "Some might be gifts."

"And the rest?"

Cassian toed off his boots and leaned against the headboard, folding his arms behind his head as his wings draped to the floor. "The females bring their jewelry. I bring my weapons."

"I know a few females in this house who might take offense to that."

Cassian offered me a wicked grin in response. The same grin

he'd given Devlon and the commanders at our meeting an hour ago. All was ready for the storm; all patrols accounted for. A standard meeting, and one I didn't need to attend, but it was always good to remind them of my presence. Especially before they all gathered for Solstice.

Azriel strode to the lone window at the end of the room and peered into the garden below. "I've never stayed in this room." His midnight voice filled the space.

"That's because you and I have been shoved to the bottom of the ladder, brother," Cassian answered, his wings draping over the bed and to the wooden floor. "Mor gets the good bedroom, Elain is living in the other, and so we get this one." He didn't mention that the final, empty bedroom—Nesta's old room—would remain open. Azriel, to his credit, didn't, either.

"Better than the attic," I offered.

"Poor Lucien," Cassian said, smiling.

"If Lucien shows up," I corrected. No word about whether he would be joining us. Or remaining in that mausoleum Tamlin called a home.

"My money's on yes," Cassian said. "Want to make a wager?"

"No," Azriel said, not turning from the window.

Cassian sat up, the portrait of outrage. "No?"

Azriel tucked in his wings. "Would *you* want people betting on you?"

"You assholes bet on me all the time. I remember the last one you did—you and Mor, making wagers about whether my wings would heal."

I snorted. True.

Azriel remained at the window. "Will Nesta stay here if she comes?"

Cassian suddenly found the Siphon atop his left hand to be in need of polishing.

I decided to spare him and said to Azriel, "Our meeting with the commanders went as well as could be expected. Devlon actually had a schedule drawn up for the girls' training, whenever this oncoming storm blows out. I don't think it was for show."

"I'd still be surprised if they remember once the storm clears," Azriel said, turning from the garden window at last.

Cassian grunted in agreement. "Anything new about the grumbling in the camps?"

I kept my face neutral. Az and I had agreed to wait until after the holiday to divulge to Cassian the full extent of what we knew, *who* we suspected or knew was behind it. We'd told him the basics, though. Enough to assuage any sort of guilt.

But I knew Cassian—as well as myself. Perhaps more so. He wouldn't be able to leave it alone if he knew now. And after all he'd been putting up with these months, and long before it, my brother deserved a break. At least for a few days.

Of course that *break* had already included the meeting with Devlon and a grueling training session atop the House of Wind this morning. Out of all of us, the concept of relaxing was the most foreign to Cassian.

Azriel leaned against the carved wood footboard at the end of his bed. "Little to add to what you already know." Smooth, easy liar. Far better than me. "But they sensed that it's growing. The best time to assess is after Solstice, when they've all returned home. See who spreads the discord then. If it's grown while they were all celebrating together or snowed in with this storm."

The perfect way to then reveal the full extent of what we knew.

If the Illyrians revolted . . . I didn't want to think that far down

145

the road. What it would cost me. What it would cost Cassian, to fight the people he still so desperately wanted to be a part of. To kill them. It'd be far different from what we'd done to the Illyrians who'd gladly served Amarantha, and done such terrible things in her name. Far different.

I shut out the thought. Later. After Solstice. We'd deal with it then.

Cassian, mercifully, seemed inclined to do the same. Not that I blamed him, given the hour of bullshit posturing he'd endured before we'd winnowed here. Even now, centuries later, the camplords and commanders still challenged him. Spat on him.

Cassian toed his own footboard, his legs not even fully stretched out. "Who used this bed anyway? It's Amren-sized."

I snorted. "Careful how you whine. Feyre calls us Illyrian babies often enough."

Azriel chuckled. "Her flying has improved enough that I think she's entitled to do so."

Pride rippled through me. Perhaps she wasn't a natural, but she made up for it with sheer grit and focus. I'd lost count of the hours we spent in the air—the precious time we'd managed to steal for ourselves.

I said to Cassian, "I can see about finding you two longer beds." With Solstice Eve here, it would take a minor miracle. I'd have to turn Velaris upside down.

He waved a hand. "No need. Better than the couch."

"You being too drunk to climb the stairs last night aside," I said wryly, earning a vulgar gesture in response, "space in this house does indeed seem to be an issue. You could stay up at the House if you'd prefer. I can winnow you in."

"The House is boring." Cassian yawned for emphasis. "Az sneaks off into shadows and I'm left all alone."

Azriel gave me a look that said, *Illyrian baby indeed*.

I hid my smile and said to Cassian, "Perhaps you should get a place of your own, then."

"I have one in Illyria."

"I meant here."

Cassian lifted a brow. "I don't need a house here. I need a *room*." He again toed the footboard, rocking the wood panel. "This one would be fine, if it didn't have a doll's bed."

I chuckled again, but held in my retort. My suggestion that he might *want* a place of his own. Soon.

Not that anything was happening on that front. Not any-time soon. Nesta had made it clear enough she had no interest in Cassian—not even in being in the same room as him. I knew why. I'd seen it happen, had felt that way plenty.

"Perhaps that will be your Solstice present, Cassian," I replied instead. "A new bed here."

"Better than Mor's presents," Az muttered.

Cassian laughed, the sound booming off the walls.

But I peered in the direction of the Sidra and lifted a brow.

+

She looked radiant.

Solstice Eve had fully settled upon Velaris, quieting the thrum that had pulsed through the city for the past few weeks, as if every-one paused to listen to the falling snow.

A gentle fall, no doubt, compared with the wild storm unleash-ing itself upon the Illyrian Mountains.

We'd gathered in the sitting room, the fire crackling, wine opened and flowing. Though neither Lucien nor Nesta had shown their faces, the mood was far from somber.

Indeed, as Feyre emerged from the kitchen hallway, I took a moment to simply drink her in from where I sat in an armchair near the fire.

She went right to Mor—perhaps because Mor was holding the wine, the bottle already outreached.

I admired the view from behind as Feyre's glass was filled.

It was an effort to leash every raging instinct at that particular view. At the curves and hollows of my mate, the color of her—so vibrant, even in this room of so many personalities. Her midnight-blue velvet gown hugged her perfectly, leaving little to the imagination before it pooled to the floor. She'd left her hair down, curling slightly at the ends—hair I knew I later wanted to plunge my hands into, scattering the silver combs pinning up the sides. And then I'd peel off that dress. Slowly.

"You'll make me vomit," Amren hissed, kicking me with her silver silk shoe from where she sat in the armchair adjacent to mine. "Rein in that scent of yours, boy."

I cut her an incredulous look. "Apologies." I threw a glance to Varian, standing to the side of her armchair, and silently offered him my condolences.

Varian, clad in Summer Court blue and gold, only grinned and inclined his head toward me.

Strange—so strange to see the Prince of Adriata here. In my town house. Smiling. Drinking my liquor.

Until—

"Do you even celebrate Solstice in the Summer Court?"

Until Cassian decided to open his mouth.

Varian turned his head toward where Cassian and Azriel lounged on the sofa, his silver hair sparkling in the firelight. "In the summer, obviously. As there are two Solstices."

Azriel hid his smile by taking a sip from his wine.

Cassian slung an arm across the back of the sofa. "Are there really?"

Mother above. It was going to be this sort of night, then.

"Don't bother answering him," Amren said to Varian, sipping from her own wine. "Cassian is precisely as stupid as he looks. And sounds," she added with a slashing glance.

Cassian lifted his glass in salute before drinking.

"I suppose your Summer Solstice is the same in theory as ours," I said to Varian, though I knew the answer. I'd seen many of them— long ago. "Families gather, food is eaten, presents shared."

Varian gave me what I could have sworn was a grateful nod. "Indeed."

Feyre appeared beside my seat, her scent settling into me. I tugged her down to perch on the rolled arm of my chair.

She did so with a familiarity that warmed something deep in me, not even bothering to look my way before her arm slid around my shoulders. Just resting there—just because she could.

Mate. My mate.

"So Tarquin doesn't celebrate Winter Solstice at all?" she asked Varian.

A shake of the head.

"Perhaps we should have invited him," Feyre mused.

"There's still time," I offered. The Cauldron knew we needed alliances more than ever. "The call is yours, Prince."

Varian peered down at Amren, who seemed to be entirely focused on her goblet of wine. "I'll think about it."

I nodded. Tarquin was his High Lord. Should he come here, Varian's focus would be elsewhere. Away from where he wished that focus to be—for the few days he had with Amren.

Mor plopped onto the sofa between Cassian and Azriel, her golden curls bouncing. "I like it to be just us anyway," she declared. "And you, Varian," she amended.

Varian offered her a smile that said he appreciated the effort.

The clock on the mantel chimed eight. As if it had summoned her, Elain slid into the room.

Mor was instantly on her feet, offering—*insisting* on wine. Typical.

Elain politely refused, taking up a spot in one of the wooden chairs set in the bay of windows. Also typical.

But Feyre was staring at the clock, her brow furrowed. *Nesta isn't coming.*

You invited her for tomorrow. I sent a soothing caress down the bond, as if it could wipe away the disappointment rippling from her.

Feyre's hand tightened on my shoulder.

I lifted my glass, the room quieting. "To family old and new. Let the Solstice festivities begin."

We all drank to that.

CHAPTER
17

Feyre

The glare of sunlight on snow filtering through our heavy velvet curtains awoke me on Solstice morning.

I scowled at the sliver of brightness and turned my head away from the window. But my cheek collided with something crinkly and firm. Definitely not my pillow.

Peeling my tongue from the roof of my mouth, rubbing at the headache that had formed by my left brow thanks to the hours of drinking, laughing, and more drinking that we'd done until the early hours of the morning, I lifted myself enough to see what had been set beside my face.

A present. Wrapped in black crepe paper and tied with silver thread. And beside it, smiling down at me, was Rhys.

He'd propped his head on a fist, his wings draped across the bed behind him. "Happy birthday, Feyre darling."

I groaned. "How are you smiling after all that wine?"

"I didn't have a whole bottle to myself, that's how." He traced a finger down the groove of my spine.

I rose onto my elbows, surveying the present he'd laid out. It was rectangular and almost flat—only an inch or two thick. "I was hoping you'd forget."

Rhys smirked. "Of course you were."

Yawning, I dragged myself into a kneeling position, stretching my arms high above my head before I pulled the gift to me. "I thought we were opening presents tonight with the others."

"It's your birthday," he drawled. "The rules don't apply to you."

I rolled my eyes at that, even as I smiled a bit. Easing away the wrapping, I pulled out a stunning notebook bound in black, supple leather, so soft it was almost like velvet. On the front, stamped in simple silver letters, were my initials.

Opening the floppy front cover, it revealed page after page of beautiful, thick paper. All blank.

"A sketchbook," he said. "Just for you."

"It's beautiful." It was. Simple, yet exquisitely made. I would have picked it for myself, had such a luxury not seemed excessive.

I leaned down to kiss him, a brush of our mouths. From the corner of my eye, I saw another item appear on my pillow.

I pulled back to see a second present waiting, the large box wrapped in amethyst paper. "More?"

Rhys waved a lazy hand, pure Illyrian arrogance. "Did you think a sketchbook would suffice for my High Lady?"

My face heating, I opened the second present. A sky-blue scarf of softest wool lay folded inside.

"So you can stop stealing Mor's," he said, winking.

I grinned, wrapping the scarf around myself. Every inch of skin it touched felt like a decadence.

"Thank you," I said, stroking the fine material. "The color is beautiful."

"Mmmm." Another wave of his hand, and a third present appeared.

"This is getting excessive."

Rhys only arched a brow, and I chuckled as I opened the third gift. "A new satchel for my painting supplies," I breathed, running my hands over the fine leather as I admired all the various pockets and straps. A set of pencils and charcoals already lay within. The front had also been monogrammed with my initials—along with a tiny Night Court insignia. "Thank you," I said again.

Rhysand's smile deepened. "I had a feeling jewels wouldn't be high on your list of desired gifts."

It was true. Beautiful as they were, I had little interest in them. And had plenty already. "This is exactly what I would have asked for."

"Had you not been hoping that your own mate would forget your birthday."

I snorted. "Had I not been hoping for that." I kissed him again, and when I made to pull away, he slid a hand behind my head and kept me there.

He kissed me deeply, lazily—as if he'd be content to do nothing but that all day. I might have considered it.

But I managed to extract myself, and crossed my legs as I settled back on the bed and reached for my new sketchbook and satchel of supplies. "I want to draw you," I said. "As my birthday present to *me*."

His smile was positively feline.

I added, flipping open my sketchbook and turning to the first page, "You said once that nude would be best."

Rhys's eyes glowed, and a whisper of his power through the room had the curtains parting, flooding the space with midmorning sunshine. Showing every glorious naked inch of him sprawled across the bed, illuminating the faint reds and golds of his wings. "Do your worst, Cursebreaker."

My very blood sparking, I pulled out a piece of charcoal and began.

✠

It was nearly eleven by the time we emerged from our room. I'd filled pages and pages of my sketchbook with him—drawings of his wings, his eyes, his Illyrian tattoos. And enough of his naked, beautiful body that I knew I'd never share this sketchbook with anyone but him. Rhys had indeed hummed his approval when he'd leafed through my work, smirking at the accuracy of my drawings regarding certain areas of his body.

The town house was still silent as we descended the stairs, my mate opting for Illyrian leathers—for whatever strange reason. If Solstice morning included one of Cassian's grueling training sessions, I'd gladly stay behind and start eating the feast I could already smell cooking in the kitchen down the hall.

Entering the dining room to find breakfast waiting, but none of our companions present, Rhys helped me into my usual seat midway down the table, then slid into the chair beside me.

"I'm assuming Mor's still asleep upstairs." I plopped a chocolate pastry onto my plate, then another onto his.

Rhys sliced into the leek-and-ham quiche and set a chunk on my plate. "She drank even more than you, so I'm guessing we won't see her until sundown."

I snorted, and held out my cup to receive the tea he now offered, steam curling from the pot's spout.

But two massive figures filled the archway of the dining room, and Rhys paused.

Azriel and Cassian, having crept up on cat-soft feet, were also wearing their Illyrian leathers.

And from their shit-eating grins, I knew this would not end well.

They moved before Rhys could, and only a flare of his power kept the teapot from falling onto the table before they hauled him out of his seat. And aimed right for the front door.

I only bit into my pastry. "Please bring him back in one piece."

"We'll take good care of him," Cassian promised, wicked humor in his eyes.

Even Azriel was still grinning as he said, "If he can keep up."

I lifted a brow, and just as they vanished out the front door, still dragging Rhys along, my mate said to me, "Tradition."

As if that was an explanation.

And then they were gone, off to the Mother knew where.

But at least neither of the Illyrians had remembered my birthday—thank the Cauldron.

So with Mor asleep and Elain likely in the kitchen helping to prepare that delicious food whose aroma now filled the house, I indulged in a rare, quiet meal. Helped myself to the pastry I'd put on Rhys's plate, along with his portion of the quiche. And another after that.

Tradition indeed.

With little to do beyond resting until the festivities began the hour before sundown, I settled in at the desk in our bedroom to do some paperwork.

Very festive, Rhys purred down the bond.

I could practically see his smirk.

And where, exactly, are you?

Don't worry about it.

I scowled at the eye on my palm, though I knew Rhys no longer used it. *That makes it sound like I should be worried.*

A dark laugh. *Cassian says you can pummel him when we get home.*

Which will be when?

A too-long pause. *Before dinner?*

I chuckled. *I really don't want to know, do I?*

You really don't.

Still smiling, I let the thread between us drop, and sighed at the papers staring up at me. Bills and letters and budgets . . .

I lifted a brow at the last, hauling a leather-bound tome toward me. A list of household expenses—just for Rhys and me. A drop of water compared with the wealth contained across his various assets. Our assets. Pulling out a piece of paper, I began counting the expenses so far, working through a tangle of mathematics.

The money *was* there—if I wanted to use it. To buy that studio. There was money in the "miscellaneous purchases" funds to do it.

Yes, I could buy that studio in a heartbeat with the fortune now in my name. But using that money so lavishly, even for a studio that wouldn't be just for me . . .

I shut the ledger, sliding my calculations into the pages, and rose. Paperwork could wait. Decisions like that could wait. Solstice, Rhys had told me, was for family. And since he was currently spending it with his brothers, I supposed I should find at least one of my sisters.

Elain met me halfway to the kitchen, bearing a tray of jam tarts toward the table in the dining room. Where an assortment of baked goods had already begun to take form, tiered cakes and iced cookies. Sugar-frosted buns and caramel-drizzled fruit pies. "Those look pretty," I told her by way of greeting, nodding toward the heart-shaped cookies on her tray. *All* of it looked pretty.

Elain smiled, her braid swishing with each step toward the growing mound of food. "They taste as good as they look." She set down the tray and wiped her flour-coated hands on the apron she wore over her dusty-pink gown. Even in the middle of winter, she was a bloom of color and sunshine.

She handed me one of the tarts, sugar sparkling. I bit in without hesitation and let out a hum of pleasure. Elain beamed.

I surveyed the food she was assembling and asked between bites, "How long have you been working on this?"

A one-shouldered shrug. "Since dawn." She added, "Nuala and Cerridwen were up hours earlier."

I'd seen the Solstice bonus Rhys had given each of them. It was more than most families made in a year. They deserved every damned copper mark.

Especially for what they'd done for my sister. The companionship, the purpose, the small sense of normalcy in that kitchen. She'd bought them those cozy, fuzzy blankets from the weaver, one raspberry pink and the other lilac.

Elain surveyed me in turn as I finished off the tart and reached for another. "Have you had any word from her?"

I knew who she meant. Just as I opened my mouth to tell her no, a knock thudded on the front door.

Elain moved fast enough that I could barely keep up, flinging open the fogged glass antechamber door in the foyer, then unlatching the heavy oak front door.

But it wasn't Nesta who stood on the front step, cheeks flushed with cold.

No, as Elain took a step back, hand falling away from the doorknob, she revealed Lucien smiling tightly at us both.

"Happy Solstice," was all he said.

CHAPTER
18

Feyre

"You look well," I said to Lucien when we'd settled in the arm-chairs before the fire, Elain perched silently on the couch nearby.

Lucien warmed his hands in the glow of the birch fire, the light casting his face in reds and golds—golds that matched his mechanical eye. "You as well." A sidelong glance toward Elain, swift and fleeting. "Both of you."

Elain said nothing, but at least she bowed her head in thanks. In the dining room, Nuala and Cerridwen continued to add food to the table, their presence now little more than twin shadows as they walked through the walls.

"You brought presents," I said uselessly, nodding toward the small stack he'd set by the window.

"It's Solstice tradition here, isn't it?"

I stifled my wince. The last Solstice I'd experienced had been at the Spring Court. With Ianthe. And Tamlin.

"You're welcome to stay for the night," I said, since Elain certainly wasn't going to.

Lucien lowered his hands into his lap and leaned back in the armchair. "Thank you, but I have other plans."

I prayed he didn't catch the slightly relieved glimmer on Elain's face.

"Where are you going?" I asked instead, hoping to keep his focus on me. Knowing it was an impossible task.

"I . . ." Lucien fumbled for the words. Not out of some lie or excuse, I realized a moment later. Realized when he said, "I've been at the Spring Court every now and then. But if I'm not here in Velaris, I've mostly been staying with Jurian. And Vassa."

I straightened. "Really? Where?"

"There's an old manor house in the southeast, in the humans' territory. Jurian and Vassa were . . . gifted it."

From the lines that bracketed his mouth, I knew who had likely arranged for the manor to fall into their hands. Graysen—or his father. I didn't dare glance at Elain.

"Rhys mentioned that they were still in Prythian. I didn't realize it was such a permanent base."

A short nod. "For now. While things are sorted out."

Like the world without a wall. Like the four human queens who still squatted across the continent. But now wasn't the time to talk of it. "How are they—Jurian and Vassa?" I'd learned enough from Rhys about how Tamlin was faring. I didn't care to hear any more of it.

"Jurian . . ." Lucien blew out a breath, scanning the carved wood ceiling above. "Thank the Cauldron for him. I never thought I'd say that, but it's true." He ran a hand through his silken red hair. "He's keeping everything running. I think he'd have been crowned king by now if it wasn't for Vassa." A twitch of the lips, a spark in that russet eye. "She's doing well enough. Savoring every second of her temporary freedom."

I had not forgotten her plea to me that night after the last battle with Hybern. To break the curse that kept her human by night, firebird by day. A once-proud queen—still proud, yes, but desperate to reclaim her freedom. Her human body. Her kingdom.

"She and Jurian are getting along?"

I hadn't seen them interact, could only imagine what the two of them would be like in the same room together. Both trying to lead the humans who occupied the sliver of land at the southernmost end of Prythian. Left ungoverned for so long. Too long.

No king or queen remained in these lands. No memory of their name, their lineage.

At least amongst humans. The Fae might know. Rhys might know.

But all that lingered of whoever had once ruled the southern tip of Prythian was a motley assortment of lords and ladies. Nothing else. No dukes or earls or any of the titles I'd once heard my sisters mention while discussing the humans on the continent. There were no such titles in the Fae lands. Not in Prythian.

No, there were just High Lords and lords. And now a High Lady.

I wondered if the humans had taken to using only *lord* as a title thanks to the High Fae who lurked above the wall.

Lurked—but no longer.

Lucien considered my question. "Vassa and Jurian are two sides of the same coin. Mercifully, their vision for the future of the human territories is mostly aligned. But the methods on how to attain that . . ." A frown to Elain, then a wince at me. "This isn't very Solstice-like talk."

Definitely not, but I didn't mind. And as for Elain . . .

My sister rose to her feet. "I should get refreshments."

Lucien rose as well. "No need to trouble yourself. I'm——"

But she was already out of the room.

When her footsteps had faded from earshot, Lucien slumped into his armchair and blew out a long breath. "How is she?"

"Better. She makes no mention of her abilities. If they remain."

"Good. But is she still . . ." A muscle flickered in his jaw. "Does she still mourn him?"

The words were little more than a growl.

I chewed on my lip, weighing how much of the truth to reveal. In the end, I opted for all of it. "She was deeply in love with him, Lucien."

His russet eye flashed with simmering rage. An uncontrollable instinct—for a mate to eliminate any threat. But he remained sitting. Even as his fingers dug into the arms of his chair.

I continued, "It has only been a few months. Graysen made it clear that the engagement is ended, but it might take her a while longer to move past it."

Again that rage. Not from jealousy, or any threat, but—"He's as fine a prick as any I've ever encountered."

Lucien *had* encountered him, I realized. Somehow, in living with Jurian and Vassa at that manor, he'd run into Elain's former betrothed. And managed to leave the human lord breathing.

"I would agree with you on that," I admitted. "But remember that they were engaged. Give her time to accept it."

"To accept a life shackled to me?"

My nostrils flared. "That's not what I meant."

"She wants nothing to do with me."

"Would *you*, if your positions were reversed?"

He didn't answer.

I tried, "After Solstice wraps up, why don't you come stay for a week or two? Not in your apartment, I mean. Here, at the town house."

"And do what?"

"Spend time with her."

"I don't think she'll tolerate two minutes alone with me, so forget about two weeks." His jaw worked as he studied the fire.

Fire. His mother's gift.

Not his father's.

Yes, it was Beron's gift. The gift of the father who the world believed had sired him. But not the gift of Helion. His true father.

I still hadn't mentioned it. To anyone other than Rhys.

Now wasn't the time for that, either.

"I'd hoped," I ventured to say, "that when you rented the apartment, it meant you would come work here. With us. Be our human emissary."

"Am I not doing that now?" He arched a brow. "Am I not sending twice-weekly reports to your spymaster?"

"You could come *live* here, is all I'm saying," I pushed. "Truly live here, stay in Velaris for longer than a few days at a time. We could get you nicer quarters—"

Lucien got to his feet. "I don't need your charity."

I rose as well. "But Jurian and Vassa's is fine?"

"You'd be surprised to see how the three of us get along."

Friends, I realized. They had somehow become his *friends*. "So you'd rather stay with them?"

"I'm not staying *with* them. The manor is *ours*."

"Interesting."

His golden eye whirred. "What is."

Not feeling very festive at all, I said sharply, "That you now feel more comfortable with humans than with the High Fae. If you ask me—"

"I'm not."

"It seems like you've decided to fall in with two people without homes of their own as well."

Lucien stared at me, long and hard. When he spoke, his voice was rough. "Happy Solstice to you, Feyre."

He turned toward the foyer, but I grabbed his arm to halt him. The corded muscle of his forearm shifted beneath the fine silk of his sapphire jacket, but he made no move to shake me off. "I didn't mean that," I said. "You have a home here. If you want it."

Lucien studied the sitting room, the foyer beyond and dining room on its other side. "The Band of Exiles."

"The what?"

"That's what we call ourselves. The Band of Exiles."

"You have a name for yourselves." I fought my incredulous tone. He nodded.

"Jurian isn't an exile," I said. Vassa, yes. Lucien, two times over now.

"Jurian's kingdom is nothing but dust and half-forgotten memory, his people long scattered and absorbed into other territories. He can call himself whatever he likes."

Yes, after the battle with Hybern, after Jurian's aid, I supposed he could.

But I asked, "And what, exactly, does this Band of Exiles plan to do? Host events? Organize party-planning committees?"

Lucien's metal eye clicked faintly and narrowed. "You can be as much of an asshole as that mate of yours, you know that?"

True. I sighed again. "I'm sorry. I just—"

"I don't have anywhere else to go." Before I could object, he said, "You ruined any chance I have of going back to Spring. Not to Tamlin, but to the court beyond his house. Everyone either still believes the lies you spun or they believe me complicit in your deceit. And as for here . . ." He shook off my grip and headed for the door. "*I* can't stand to be in the same room as her for more than two minutes. *I* can't stand to be in this court and have your mate pay for the very clothes on my back."

I studied the jacket he wore. I'd seen it before. Back in—

"Tamlin sent it to our manor yesterday," Lucien hissed. "My clothes. My belongings. All of it. He had it sent from the Spring Court and dumped on the doorstep."

Bastard. Still a bastard, despite what he'd done for Rhys and me during that last battle. But the blame for that behavior was not on Tamlin's shoulders alone. I'd created that rift. Ripped it apart with my own two hands.

I didn't quite feel guilty enough to warrant apologizing for it. Not yet. Possibly not ever.

"Why?" It was the only question I could think to ask.

"Perhaps it had something to do with your mate's visit the other day."

My spine stiffened. "Rhys didn't involve you in that."

"He might as well have. Whatever he said or did, Tamlin decided he wishes to remain in solitude." His russet eye darkened. "Your mate should have known better than to kick a downed male."

"I can't say I'm particularly sorry that he did."

"You will need Tamlin as an ally before the dust has settled. Tread carefully."

I didn't want to think about it, consider it, today. Any day. "My business with him is done."

"Yours might be, but Rhys's isn't. And you'd do well to remind your mate of that fact."

A pulse down the bond, as if in answer. *Everything all right?*

I let Rhys see and hear all that had been said, the conversation conveyed in the blink of an eye. *I'm sorry to have caused him trouble*, Rhys said. *Do you need me to come home?*

I'll handle it.

Let me know if you need anything, Rhys said, and the bond went silent.

"Checking in?" Lucien asked quietly.

"I don't know what you're talking about," I said, my face the portrait of boredom.

He gave me a knowing look, continuing to the door and grabbing his heavy overcoat and scarf from the hooks mounted on the wood paneling beside it. "The bigger box is for you. The smaller one is for her."

It took me a heartbeat to realize he meant the presents. I glanced over my shoulder to the careful silver wrapping, the blue bows atop both boxes.

When I looked back, Lucien was gone.

✤

I found my sister in the kitchen, watching the kettle scream.

"He's not staying for tea," I said.

No sign of Nuala or Cerridwen.

Elain simply removed the kettle from the heat.

I knew I wasn't truly angry with her, not angry with anyone but myself, but I said, "You couldn't say a single word to him? A pleasant greeting?"

Elain only stared at the steaming kettle as she set it on the stone counter.

"He brought you a present."

Those doe-brown eyes turned toward me. Sharper than I'd ever seen them. "And that entitles him to my time, my affections?"

"No." I blinked. "But he is a *good* male." Despite our harsh words. Despite this Band of Exiles bullshit. "He cares for you."

"He doesn't know me."

"You don't give him the chance to even try to do so."

Her mouth tightened, the only sign of anger in her graceful countenance. "I don't want a mate. I don't want a *male*."

She wanted a human man.

Solstice. Today was Solstice, and everyone was supposed to be cheerful and happy. Certainly *not* fighting left and right. "I know you don't." I loosed a long breath. "But . . ."

But I had no idea how to finish that sentence. Just because Lucien was her mate didn't mean he had a claim on her time. Her affection. She was her own person, capable of making her own choices. Assessing her own needs.

"He is a good male," I repeated. "And it . . . it just . . ." I fought for the words. "I don't like to see either of you unhappy."

Elain stared at the worktable, baked goods both finished and incomplete arrayed on the surface, the kettle now cooling on the counter. "I know you don't."

There was nothing else to be said. So I touched her shoulder and strode out.

Elain didn't say a word.

I found Mor sitting on the bottom steps of the stairs, wearing a pair of peach-colored loose pants and a heavy white sweater. A combination of Amren's usual style and my own.

Gold earrings flashing, Mor offered a grim smile. "Drink?" A decanter and pair of glasses appeared in her hands.

"Mother above, yes."

She waited until I'd sat beside her on the oak steps and downed a mouthful of amber liquid, the stuff burning its way along my throat and warming my belly, before she asked, "Do you want my advice?"

No. Yes.

I nodded.

Mor drank deeply from her glass. "Stay out of it. She's not ready, and neither is he, no matter how many presents he brings."

I lifted a brow. "Snoop."

Mor leaned back against the steps, utterly unrepentant. "Let him live with his Band of Exiles. Let him deal with Tamlin in his own way. Let him figure out where he wants to be. *Who* he wants to be. The same goes with her."

She was right.

"I know you still blame yourself for your sisters being Made." Mor nudged my knee with her own. "And because of that, you want to fix everything for them now that they're here."

"I always wanted to do that," I said glumly.

Mor smiled crookedly. "That's why we love you. Why they love you."

Nesta, I wasn't so sure about.

Mor continued, "Just be patient. It'll sort itself out. It always does."

Another kernel of truth.

I refilled my glass, set the crystal decanter on the step behind us, and drank again. "I want them to be happy. All of them."

"They will be."

She said the simple words with such unflagging conviction that I believed her.

I arched a brow. "And you—are you happy?"

Mor knew what I meant. But she just smiled, swirling the liquor in her glass. "It's Solstice. I'm with my family. I'm drinking. I'm *very* happy."

A skilled evasion. But one I was content to partake in. I clinked my heavy glass against hers. "Speaking of our family . . . Where the *hell* are they?"

Mor's brown eyes lit up. "Oh—oh, he didn't tell you, did he?"

My smile faltered. "Tell me what."

"What the three of them do every Solstice morning."

"I'm beginning to be nervous."

Mor set down her glass, and gripped my arm. "Come with me."

Before I could object, she'd winnowed us out.

Blinding light hit me. And cold.

Brisk, brutal cold. Far too cold for the sweaters and pants we wore.

Snow. And sun. And wind.

And mountains.

And—a cabin.

The cabin.

Mor pointed to the endless field atop the mountain. Covered in snow, just as I'd last seen it. But rather than a flat, uninterrupted expanse . . .

"Are those *snow forts?*"

A nod.

Something white shot across the field, white and hard and glistening, and then—

Cassian's yowl echoed off the mountains around us. Followed by, "You *bastard*!"

Rhys's answering laugh was bright as the sun on snow.

I surveyed the three walls of snow—the *barricades*—that bordered the field as Mor erected an invisible shield against the bitter wind. It did little to drive away the cold, though. "They're having a snowball fight."

Another nod.

"Three Illyrian warriors," I said. "The *greatest* Illyrian warriors. Are having a snowball fight."

Mor's eyes practically glowed with wicked delight. "Since they were children."

"They're over five hundred years old."

"Do you want me to tell you the running tally of victories?"

I gaped at her. Then at the field beyond. At the snowballs that were indeed flying with brutal, swift precision as dark heads popped over the walls they'd built.

"No magic," Mor recited, "no wings, no breaks."

"They've been out here since noon." It was nearly three. My teeth began chattering.

"I've always stayed in to drink," Mor supplied, as if that were an answer.

"How do they even decide who *wins?*"

"Whoever doesn't get frostbite?"

I gaped at her again over my clacking teeth. "This is ridiculous."

"There's more alcohol in the cabin."

Indeed, none of the males seemed to even notice us. Not as Azriel popped up, launched two snowballs sky-high, and vanished behind his wall of snow again.

A moment later, Rhys's vicious curse barked toward us. *"Asshole."*

Laughter laced every syllable.

Mor looped her arm through mine again. "I don't think your mate is going to be the victor this year, my friend."

I leaned into her warmth, and we waded through the shin-high snow toward the cabin, the chimney already puffing against the clear blue sky.

Illyrian babies indeed.

CHAPTER
19

Feyre

Azriel won.

His one-hundred-ninety-ninth victory, apparently.

The three of them had entered the cabin an hour later, dripping snow, skin splotched with red, grinning from ear to ear.

Mor and I, snuggled together beneath a blanket on the couch, only rolled our eyes at them.

Rhys just dropped a kiss atop my head, declared the three of them were going to take a steam in the cedar-lined shed attached to the house, and then they were gone.

I blinked at Mor as they vanished, letting the image settle.

"Another tradition," she told me, the bottle of amber-colored alcohol mostly empty. And my head now spinning with it. "An Illyrian custom, actually—the heated sheds. The birchin. A bunch of naked warriors, sitting together in the steam, sweating."

I blinked again.

Mor's lips twitched. "About the only good custom the Illyrians ever came up with, to be honest."

I snorted. "So the three of them are just in there. Naked. Sweating."

Mother above.

Interested in taking a look? The dark purr echoed into my mind.

Lech. Go back to your sweating.

There's room for one more in here.

I thought mates were territorial.

I could feel him smile as if he were grinning against my neck. *I'm always eager to learn what sparks your interest, Feyre darling.*

I surveyed the cabin around me, the surfaces I'd painted nearly a year ago. *I was promised a wall, Rhys.*

A pause. A long pause. *I've taken you against a wall before.*

These walls.

Another long, long pause. *It's bad form to be at attention while in the birchin.*

My lips curved as I sent him an image. A memory.

Of me on the kitchen table just a few feet away. Of him kneeling before me. My legs wrapped around his head.

Cruel, wicked thing.

I heard a door slamming somewhere in the house, followed by a distinctly male yelp. Then banging—as if someone was trying to get back inside.

Mor's eyes sparkled. "You got him kicked out, didn't you?"

My answering smile set her roaring.

⁜

The sun was sinking toward the distant sea beyond Velaris when Rhys stood at the black marble mantel of the town house sitting room and lifted his glass of wine.

All of us—in our finery for once—lifted ours in suit.

I'd opted to wear my Starfall gown, forgoing my crown but wearing the diamond cuffs at my wrists. It sparkled and gleamed in my line of vision as I stood at Rhys's side, taking in every plane of his beautiful face as he said, "To the blessed darkness from which we are born, and to which we return."

Our glasses rose, and we drank.

I glanced to him—my mate, in his finest black jacket, the silver embroidery gleaming in the faelight. *That's it?*

He arched a brow. *Did you want me to keep droning on, or did you want to start celebrating?*

My lips twitched. *You really do keep things casual.*

Even after all this time, you still don't believe me. His hand slid behind me and pinched. I bit my lip to keep from laughing. *I hope you got me a good Solstice present.*

It was my turn to pinch him, and Rhys laughed, kissing my temple once before sauntering out of the room to no doubt grab more wine.

Beyond the windows, darkness had indeed fallen. The longest night of the year.

I found Elain studying it, beautiful in her amethyst-colored gown. I made to move toward her, but someone beat me to it.

The shadowsinger was clad in a black jacket and pants similar to Rhysand's—the fabric immaculately tailored and built to fit his wings. He still wore his Siphons atop either hand, and shadows trailed his footsteps, curling like swirled embers, but there was little sign of the warrior otherwise. Especially as he gently said to my sister, "Happy Solstice."

Elain turned from the snow falling in the darkness beyond and smiled slightly. "I've never participated in one of these."

Amren supplied from across the room, Varian at her side, resplendent in his princely regalia, "They're highly overrated."

Mor smirked. "Says the female who makes out like a bandit every year. I don't know how you don't get robbed going home with so much jewelry stuffed into your pockets."

Amren flashed her too-white teeth. "Careful, Morrigan, or I'll return the pretty little thing I got you."

Mor, to my surprise, shut right up.

And so did the others, as Rhys returned with—

"You didn't." I blurted out the words.

He grinned at me over the giant tiered cake in his arms—over the twenty-one sparkling candles lighting up his face.

Cassian clapped me on the shoulder. "You thought you could sneak it past us, didn't you?"

I groaned. "You're all insufferable."

Elain floated to my side. "Happy birthday, Feyre."

My friends—my family—echoed the words as Rhys set the cake on the low-lying table before the fire. I glanced toward my sister. "Did you . . . ?"

A nod from Elain. "Nuala did the decorating, though."

It was then that I realized what the three different tiers had been painted to look like.

On the top: flowers. In the middle: flames.

And on the bottom, widest layer . . . stars.

The same design of the chest of drawers I'd once painted in that dilapidated cottage. One for each of us—each sister. Those stars and moons sent to me, my mind, by my mate, long before we'd ever met.

"I asked Nuala to do it in that order," Elain said as the others gathered round. "Because you're the foundation, the one who lifts us. You always have been."

My throat tightened unbearably, and I squeezed her hand in answer.

Mor, Cauldron bless her, shouted, "Make a wish and let us get to the presents!"

At least one tradition did not change on either side of the wall.

I met Rhys's stare over the sparkling candles. His smile was enough to make the tightness in my throat turn into burning in my eyes.

What are you going to wish for?

A simple, honest question.

And looking at him, at that beautiful face and easy smile, so many of those shadows vanished, our family gathered around us, eternity a road ahead . . . I knew.

I truly knew what I wanted to wish for, as if it were a piece of Amren's puzzle clicking into place, as if the threads of the weaver's tapestry finally revealed the design they'd formed to make.

I didn't tell him, though. Not as I gathered my breath and blew.

✢

Cake before dinner was utterly acceptable on Solstice, Rhys informed me as we set aside our plates on whatever surface was nearest in the sitting room. Especially before presents.

"What presents?" I asked, surveying the room empty of them, save for Lucien's two boxes.

The others grinned at me as Rhys snapped his fingers, and—

"Oh."

Boxes and bags, all brightly wrapped and adorned, filled the bay windows.

Piles and mountains and *towers* of them. Mor let out a squeal of delight.

I twisted toward the foyer. I'd left mine in a broom closet on the third level—

No. There they were. Wrapped and by the back of the bay.

Rhys winked at me. "I took it upon myself to add your presents to the communal trove."

I lifted my brows. "Everyone gave you their gifts?"

"He's the only one who can be trusted not to snoop," Mor explained.

I looked toward Azriel.

"Even him," Amren said.

Azriel gave me a guilty cringe. "Spymaster, remember?"

"We started doing it two centuries ago," Mor went on. "After Rhys caught Amren literally *shaking* a box to figure out what was inside."

Amren clicked her tongue as I laughed. "What they didn't see was Cassian down here ten minutes earlier, *sniffing* each box."

Cassian threw her a lazy smile. "I wasn't the one who got caught."

I turned to Rhys. "And somehow *you're* the most trustworthy one?"

Rhys looked outright offended. "I am a High Lord, Feyre darling. Unwavering honor is built into my bones."

Mor and I snorted.

Amren strode for the nearest pile of presents. "I'll go first."

"Of course she will," Varian muttered, earning a grin from me and Mor.

Amren smiled sweetly at him before bending to pick up a gift. Varian had the good sense to shudder only when she'd turned her back on him.

But she plucked up a pink-wrapped present, read the label, and ripped into it.

Everyone tried and failed to hide their wince.

I'd seen some animals tear into carcasses with less ferocity.

But she beamed as she turned to Azriel, a set of exquisite pearl-and-diamond earrings dangling from her small hands. "Thank you, Shadowsinger," she said, inclining her head.

Azriel only inclined his head in return. "I'm glad they pass inspection."

Cassian elbowed his way past Amren, earning a hiss of warning, and began chucking presents. Mor caught hers easily, shredding the paper with as much enthusiasm as Amren. She grinned at the general. "Thank you, darling."

Cassian smirked. "I know what you like."

Mor held up—

I choked. Azriel did, too, whirling on Cassian as he did.

Cassian only winked at him as the barely there red negligee swayed between Mor's hands.

Before Azriel could undoubtedly ask what we were all thinking, Mor hummed to herself and said, "Don't let him fool you: he couldn't think of a damn thing to get me, so he gave up and asked me outright. I gave him precise orders. For once in his life, he obeyed them."

"The perfect warrior, through and through," Rhys drawled.

Cassian leaned back on the couch, stretching his long legs before him. "Don't worry, Rhysie. I got one for you, too."

"Shall I model it for you?"

I laughed, surprised to hear the sound echo across the room. From Elain.

Her present . . . I hurried to the pile of gifts before Cassian could lob one across the room again, hunting for the parcel I'd carefully wrapped yesterday. I just spied it behind a larger box when I heard it. The knock.

Just once. Quick and hard.

I knew. I knew, before Rhys even looked toward me, who was standing at that door.

Everyone did.

Silence fell, interrupted only by the crackling fire.

A beat, and then I was moving, dress swishing around me as I crossed into the foyer, heaved open the leaded glass door and the oak one beyond it, then braced myself against the onslaught of cold.

Against the onslaught of Nesta.

CHAPTER
20

Feyre

Snow clung to Nesta's hair as we stared at each other across the threshold.

Pink tinged her cheeks from the frigid night, but her face remained solemn. Cold as the snow-dusted cobblestones.

I opened the door a bit wider. "We're in the sitting room."

"I saw."

Conversation, tentative and halting, carried to the foyer. No doubt a noble attempt by everyone to give us some privacy and sense of normalcy.

When Nesta remained on the doorstep, I extended a hand toward her. "Here—I'll take your coat."

I tried not to hold my breath as she glanced past me, into the house. As if weighing whether to take that step over the threshold.

From the edge of my vision, purple and gold flashed—Elain. "You'll fall ill if you just stand there in the cold," she tutted to Nesta, smiling broadly. "Come sit with me by the fire."

Nesta's blue-gray eyes slid to mine. Wary. Assessing.

I held my ground. Held that door open.

Without a word, my sister crossed the threshold.

It was the matter of a moment to remove her coat, scarf, and gloves to reveal one of those simple yet elegant gowns she favored. She'd opted for a slate gray. No jewelry. Certainly no presents, but at least she'd come.

Elain linked elbows to lead Nesta into the room, and I followed, watching the group beyond as they paused.

Watching Cassian especially, now standing with Az at the fire.

He was the portrait of relaxed, an arm braced against the carved mantel, his wings tucked in loosely, a faint grin on his face and a glass of wine in his hand. He slid his hazel eyes toward my sister without him moving an inch.

Elain had plastered a smile onto her face as she led Nesta not toward the fire as she'd promised, but the liquor cabinet.

"Don't take her to the wine—take her to the food," Amren called to Elain from her perch on the armchair as she slid the pearl earrings Az had given her into her lobes. "I can see her bony ass even through that dress."

Nesta halted halfway across the room, spine stiff. Cassian went still as death.

Elain paused beside our sister, that plastered-on smile faltering.

Amren just smirked at Nesta. "Happy Solstice, girl."

Nesta stared at Amren—until a ghost of a smile curved her lips. "Pretty earrings."

I felt, more than saw, the room relax slightly.

Elain said brightly, "We were just getting to presents."

It occurred to me only when she said the words that none of the gifts in this room had Nesta's name on them.

"We haven't eaten yet," I supplied, lingering in the threshold between the sitting room and foyer. "But if you're hungry, we can get you a plate—"

Nesta accepted the glass of wine Elain pressed into her hand. I didn't fail to note that when Elain turned again to the liquor cabinet, she poured a finger of amber-colored liquor into a glass and knocked back the contents with a grimace before facing Nesta again.

A soft snort from Amren at that, missing nothing.

But Nesta's attention had gone to the birthday cake still sitting on the table, its various tiers delved into many times over.

Her eyes lifted to mine in the silence. "Happy birthday."

I offered a nod of thanks. "Elain made the cake," I offered somewhat uselessly.

Nesta only nodded before heading for a chair near the back of the room, by one of the bookcases. "You can return to your presents," she said softly, but not weakly, as she sat.

Elain rushed toward a box near the front of the pile. "This one's for you," she declared to our sister.

I threw Rhys a pleading glance. *Please start talking again. Please.*

Some of the light had vanished from his violet eyes as he studied Nesta while she drank from her glass. He didn't respond down the bond, but instead said to Varian, "Does Tarquin host a formal party for the Summer Solstice, or does he have a more casual gathering?"

The Prince of Adriata didn't miss a beat, and launched into a perhaps unnecessarily detailed description of the Summer Court's celebrations. I'd thank him for it later.

Elain had reached Nesta by then, offering her what seemed to be a heavy, paper-wrapped box.

By the windows, Mor sprang into motion, handing Azriel his gift.

Torn between watching the two, I remained in the doorway.

Azriel's composure didn't so much as falter as he opened her present: a set of embroidered blue towels—with his initials on them. Bright blue.

I had to look away to keep from laughing. Az, to his credit, gave Mor a smile of thanks, a blush creeping over his cheeks, his hazel eyes fixed on her. I looked away at the heat, the yearning that filled them.

But Mor waved him off and moved to pass Cassian his gift; but the warrior didn't take it. Or take his eyes off Nesta as she undid the brown paper wrapping on the box and revealed a set of five novels in a leather box. She read the titles, then lifted her head to Elain.

Elain smiled down at her. "I went into that bookshop. You know the one by the theater? I asked them for recommendations, and the woman—female, I mean . . . She said this author's books were her favorite."

I inched close enough to read one of the titles. Romance, from the sound of it.

Nesta pulled out one of the books and fanned through the pages. "Thank you."

The words were stiff—gravelly.

Cassian at last turned to Mor, tearing open her present with a disregard for the fine wrapping. He laughed at whatever was inside the box. "Just what I always wanted." He held up a pair of what seemed to be red silk undershorts. The perfect match to her negligee.

With Nesta pointedly preoccupied with flipping through her new books, I moved to the presents I'd wrapped yesterday.

For Amren: a specially designed folding carrier for her puzzles. So she didn't need to leave them at home if she were to visit sunnier, warmer lands. This earned me both an eye roll and a smile of appreciation. The ruby-and-silver brooch, shaped like a pair of feathered wings, earned me a rare peck on the cheek.

For Elain: a pale blue cloak with armholes, perfect for gardening in the chillier months.

And for Cassian, Azriel, and Mor . . .

I grunted as I hauled over the three wrapped paintings. Then waited in foot-shifting silence while they opened them.

While they beheld what was inside and smiled.

I hadn't any idea what to get them, other than this. The pieces I'd worked on recently—glimpses of their stories.

None of them explained what the paintings meant, what they beheld. But each of them kissed me on the cheek in thanks.

Before I could hand Rhys his present, I found a heap of them in my lap.

From Amren: an illuminated manuscript, ancient and beautiful. From Azriel: rare, vibrant paint from the continent. From Cassian: a proper leather sheath for a blade, to be set down the groove of my spine like a true Illyrian warrior. From Elain: fine brushes monogrammed with my initials and the Night Court insignia on the handles. And from Mor: a pair of fleece-lined slippers. Bright pink, fleece-lined slippers.

Nothing from Nesta, but I didn't care. Not one bit.

The others passed around their gifts, and I finally found a moment to haul the last painting over to Rhys. He'd lingered by the bay window, quiet and smiling. Last year had been his first Solstice since Amarantha—this year, his second. I didn't want to know what it had been like, what she'd done to him, during those forty-nine Solstices he'd missed.

Rhys opened my present carefully, lifting the painting so the others wouldn't see it.

I watched his eyes rove over what was on it. Watched his throat bob.

"Tell me that's not your new pet," Cassian said, having snuck behind me to peer at it.

I shoved him away. "Snoop."

Rhys's face remained solemn, his eyes star-bright as they met mine. "Thank you."

The others continued on a tad more loudly—to give us privacy in that crowded room.

"I have no idea where you might hang it," I said, "but I wanted you to have it."

To see.

For on that painting, I'd shown him what I had not revealed to anyone. What the Ouroboros had revealed to me: the creature inside myself, the creature full of hate and regret and love and sacrifice, the creature that could be cruel and brave, sorrowful and joyous.

I gave him *me*—as no one but him would ever see me. No one but him would ever understand.

"It's beautiful," he said, voice still hoarse.

I blinked away the tears that threatened at those words and leaned into the kiss he pressed to my mouth. *You are beautiful*, he whispered down the bond.

So are you.

I know.

I laughed, pulling away. *Prick.*

There were only a few presents left—Lucien's. I opened mine to find a gift for me and my mate: three bottles of fine liquor. *You'll need it*, was all the note said.

I handed Elain the small box with her name on it. Her smile faded as she opened it.

"Enchanted gloves," she read from the card. "That won't tear or become too sweaty while gardening." She set aside the box without looking at it for longer than a moment. And I wondered if she *preferred* to have torn and sweaty hands, if the dirt and cuts were proof of her labor. Her joy.

Amren squealed—actually *squealed*—with delight when she beheld Rhys's present. The jewels glittering inside the multiple boxes. But her delight turned quieter, more tender when she opened Varian's gift. She didn't show any of us what was inside the small box before offering him a small, private smile.

There was a tiny box left on the table by the window—a box that Mor lifted, squinted at the name tag, and said, "Az, this one's for you."

The shadowsinger's brows lifted, but his scarred hand extended to take the present.

Elain turned from where she'd been speaking to Nesta. "Oh, that's from me."

Azriel's face didn't so much as shift at the words. Not even a smile as he opened the present and revealed—

"I had Madja make it for me," Elain explained. Azriel's brows narrowed at the mention of the family's preferred healer. "It's a powder to mix in with any drink."

Silence.

Elain bit her lip and then smiled sheepishly. "It's for the headaches everyone always gives you. Since you rub your temples so often."

Silence again.

Then Azriel tipped his head back and *laughed*.

I'd never heard such a sound, deep and joyous. Cassian and Rhys joined him, the former grabbing the glass bottle from Azriel's hand and examining it. "Brilliant," Cassian said.

Elain smiled again, ducking her head.

Azriel mastered himself enough to say, "Thank you." I'd never seen his hazel eyes so bright, the hues of green amid the brown and gray like veins of emerald. "This will be invaluable."

"Prick," Cassian said, but laughed again.

Nesta watched warily from her chair, Elain's present—her only present—in her lap. Her spine stiffened slightly. Not at the words, but at Elain, laughing with them. With us.

As if Nesta were looking at us through some sort of window. As if she were still standing out in the front yard, watching us in the house.

I forced myself to smile, though. To laugh with them.

I had a feeling Cassian was doing the same.

⊹

The night was a blur of laughter and drinking, even with Nesta sitting in near-silence at the packed dinner table.

It was only when the clock chimed two that the yawns began to appear. Amren and Varian were the first to leave, the latter bearing all of her presents in his arms, the former nestled in the fine ermine

187

coat that he'd given her—a second gift to whatever one he'd put in that small box.

Settled again in the sitting room, Nesta got to her feet half an hour later. She quietly bid Elain good night, dropping a kiss to the top of her hair, and drifted for the front door.

Cassian, nestled with Mor, Rhys, and Azriel on the couch, didn't so much as move.

But I did, rising from my own chair to follow Nesta to where she was donning her layers at the front door. I waited until she'd entered the antechamber before extending my hand.

"Here."

Nesta half turned toward me, focus darting to what was in my hand. The small slip of paper.

The banker's note for her rent. And then some.

"As promised," I said.

For a moment, I prayed she wouldn't take it. That she would tell me to tear it up.

But Nesta's lips only tightened, her fingers unwavering as she took the money.

As she turned her back on me and walked out the front door, into the freezing darkness beyond.

I remained in the chilly antechamber, hand still outstretched, the phantom dryness of that check lingering on my fingers.

The floorboards thudded behind me, and then I was being gently but forcibly moved to the side. It happened so fast I barely had time to realize that Cassian had gone storming past—right out the front door.

To my sister.

CHAPTER
21

Cassian

He'd had enough.

Enough of the coldness, the sharpness. Enough of the sword-straight spine and razor-sharp stare that had only honed itself these months.

Cassian could barely hear over the roaring in his head as he charged into the snowy night. Could barely register moving aside his High Lady to get to the front door. To get to Nesta.

She'd already made it to the gate, walking with that unfaltering grace despite the icy ground. Her collection of books tucked under an arm.

It was only when Cassian reached her that he realized he had nothing to say. Nothing to say that wouldn't make her laugh in his face.

"I'll walk you home," was all that came out instead.

Nesta paused just past the low iron gate, her face cold and pale as moonlight.

Beautiful. Even with the weight loss, she was as beautiful

standing in the snow as she'd been the first time he'd laid eyes on her in her father's house.

And infinitely more deadly. In so many ways.

She looked him over. "I'm fine."

"It's a long walk, and it's late."

And you didn't say one gods-damned word to me the entire night.

Not that he'd said a word to her.

She'd made it clear enough in those initial days after that last battle that she wanted nothing to do with him. With any of them.

He understood. He really did. It had taken him months—*years*—after his first battles to readjust. To cope. Hell, he was still reeling from what had happened in that final battle with Hybern, too.

Nesta held her ground, proud as any Illyrian. More vicious, too. "Go back into the house."

Cassian gave her a crooked grin, one he knew sent that temper of hers boiling. "I think I need some fresh air, anyway."

She rolled her eyes and launched into a walk. He wasn't stupid enough to offer to carry her books.

Instead, he easily kept pace, an eye out for any treacherous patches of ice on the cobblestones. They'd barely survived Hybern. He didn't need her snapping her neck on the street.

Nesta lasted all of a block, the green-roofed houses merry and still full of song and laughter, before she halted. Whirled on him.

"Go back to the house."

"I will," he said, flashing a grin again. "After I drop you off at your front door."

At that piece-of-shit apartment she insisted on living in. Across the city.

Nesta's eyes—the same as Feyre's and yet wholly different, sharp and cold as steel—went to his hands. What was in them. "What is that."

Another grin as he lifted the small, wrapped parcel. "Your Solstice present."

"I don't want one."

Cassian continued past her, tossing the present in his hands. "You'll want this one."

He prayed she would. It had taken him months to find it.

He hadn't wanted to give it to her in front of the others. Hadn't even known she'd be there tonight. He'd been well aware of Elain's and Feyre's cajoling. Just as he'd been well aware of the money he'd seen Feyre give to Nesta moments before she left.

As promised, his High Lady had said.

He wished she hadn't. Wished for a lot of things.

Nesta fell into step beside him, huffing as she kept up with his long strides. "I don't want *anything* from you."

He made himself arch an eyebrow. "You sure about that, sweetheart?"

I have no regrets in my life, but this. That we did not have time.

Cassian shut out the words. Shut out the image that chased him from his dreams, night after night: not Nesta holding up the King of Hybern's head like a trophy; not the way her father's neck had twisted in Hybern's hands. But the image of her leaning over him, *covering* Cassian's body with her own, ready to take the full brunt of the king's power for him. To die for him—with him. That slender, beautiful body, arching over him, shaking in terror, willing to face that end.

He hadn't seen a glimpse of that person in months. Had not seen her smile or laugh.

He knew about the drinking, about the males. He told himself he didn't care.

He told himself he didn't want to know who the bastard was who had taken her maidenhead. Told himself he didn't want to know if the males meant anything—if *he* meant anything.

He didn't know why the hell he cared. Why he'd bothered. Even from the start. Even after she'd kneed him in the balls that one afternoon at her father's house.

Even as she said, "I've made my thoughts clear enough on what I want from *you*."

He'd never met someone able to imply so much in so few words, in placing so much emphasis on *you* as to make it an outright insult.

Cassian clenched his jaw. And didn't bother to restrain himself when he said, "I'm tired of playing these bullshit games."

She kept her chin high, the portrait of queenly arrogance. "I'm not."

"Well, everyone else is. Perhaps you can find it in yourself to try a little harder this year."

Those striking eyes slid toward him, and it was an effort to stand his ground. "Try?"

"I know that's a foreign word to you."

Nesta stopped at the bottom of the street, right along the icy Sidra. "Why should I have to *try* to do anything?" Her teeth flashed. "I was dragged into this world of yours, this court."

"Then go somewhere else."

Her mouth formed a tight line at the challenge. "Perhaps I will."

But he knew there was no other place to go. Not when she had no money, no family beyond this territory. "Be sure to write."

She launched into a walk again, keeping along the river's edge.

Cassian followed, hating himself for it. "You could at least come live at the House," he began, and she whirled on him.

"*Stop*," she snarled.

He halted in his tracks, wings spreading slightly to balance him.

"*Stop* following me. *Stop* trying to haul me into your happy little circle. *Stop doing all of it.*"

He knew a wounded animal when he saw one. Knew the teeth they could bare, the viciousness they displayed. But it couldn't keep him from saying, "Your sisters love you. I can't for the life of me understand why, but they do. If you can't be bothered to try for my happy little circle's sake, then at least try for them."

A void seemed to enter those eyes. An endless, depthless void. She only said, "Go home, Cassian."

He could count on one hand the number of times she'd used his name. Called him anything other than *you* or *that one*.

She turned away—toward her apartment, her grimy part of the city.

It was instinct to lunge for her free hand.

Her gloved fingers scraped against his calluses, but he held firm. "Talk to me. Nesta. Tell me—"

She ripped her hand out of his grip. Stared him down. A mighty, vengeful queen.

He waited, panting, for the verbal lashing to begin. For her to shred him into ribbons.

But Nesta only stared at him, her nose crinkling. Stared, then snorted—and walked away.

As if he were nothing. As if he weren't worth her time. The effort.

A low-born Illyrian bastard.

This time, when she continued onward, Cassian didn't follow.

He watched her until she was a shadow against the darkness—and then she vanished completely.

He remained staring after her, that present in his hands.

Cassian's fingertips dug into the soft wood of the small box.

He was grateful the streets were empty when he hurled that box into the Sidra. Hurled it hard enough that the splash echoed off the buildings flanking the river, ice cracking from the impact.

Ice instantly re-formed over the hole he'd blown open. As if it, and the present, had never been.

Nesta

Nesta sealed the fourth and final lock on her apartment door and slumped against the creaking, rotting wood.

Silence settled in around her, welcome and smothering.

Silence, to soothe the trembling that had chased her across this city.

He'd followed.

She'd known it in her bones, her blood. He'd kept high in the skies, but he'd followed until she'd entered the building.

She knew he was now waiting on a nearby rooftop to see her light kindle.

Twin instincts warred within her: to leave the faelight untouched and make him wait in the freezing dark, or to ignite that bowl and just get rid of his presence. Get rid of everything he was.

She opted for the latter.

In the dim, thick silence, Nesta lingered by the table against the wall near her front door. Slid her hand into her pocket and pulled out the folded banknote.

Enough for three months' rent.

She tried and failed to muster the shame. But nothing came.

Nothing at all.

There was anger, occasionally. Sharp, hot anger that sliced her.

But most of the time it was silence.

Ringing, droning silence.

She hadn't felt anything in months. Had days when she didn't really know where she was or what she'd done. They passed swiftly and yet dripped by.

So did the months. She'd blinked, and winter had fallen. Blinked, and her body had turned too thin. As hollow as she felt.

The night's frosty chill crept through the worn shutters, drawing another tremble from her. But she didn't light the fire in the hearth across the room.

She could barely stand to hear the crack and pop of the wood. Had barely been able to endure it in Feyre's town house. *Snap; crunch.*

How no one ever remarked that it sounded like breaking bones, like a snapping neck, she had no idea.

She hadn't lit one fire in this apartment. Had kept warm with blankets and layers.

Wings rustled, then boomed outside the apartment.

Nesta loosed a shuddering sigh and slid down the wall until she was sitting against it.

Until she drew her knees to her chest and stared into the dimness.

Still the silence raged and echoed around her.

Still she felt nothing.

CHAPTER
22

Feyre

It was three by the time the others went to bed. By the time Cassian returned, quiet and brooding, and knocked back a glass of liquor before stalking upstairs. Mor followed him, worry dancing in her eyes.

Azriel and Elain remained in the sitting room, my sister showing him the plans she'd sketched to expand the garden in the back of the town house, using the seeds and tools my family had given her tonight. Whether he cared about such things, I had no idea, but I sent him a silent prayer of thanks for his kindness before Rhys and I slipped upstairs.

I reached to remove my diamond cuffs when Rhys stopped me, his hands wrapping around my wrists. "Not yet," he said softly.

My brows bunched.

He only smiled. "Hold on."

Darkness and wind swept in, and I clung to him as he winnowed—

Candlelight and crackling fire and colors . . .

"The cabin?" He must have altered the wards to allow us to winnow directly inside.

Rhys grinned, letting go of me to swagger to the couch before the fireplace and plop down, his wings draping to the floor. "For some peace and quiet, mate."

Dark, sensual promise lay in his star-flecked eyes.

I bit my lip as I approached the rolled arm of the couch and perched on it, my dress glittering like a river in the firelight.

"You look beautiful tonight." His words were low, rough.

I stroked a hand down the lap of my gown, the fabric shimmering beneath my fingers. "You say that every night."

"And mean it."

I blushed. "Cad."

He inclined his head.

"I know High Ladies are probably supposed to wear a new dress every day," I mused, smiling at the gown, "but I'm rather attached to this one."

He ran his hand down my thigh. "I'm glad."

"You never told me where you got it—where you got all my favorite dresses."

Rhys arched a dark brow. "You never figured it out?"

I shook my head.

For a moment, he said nothing, his head dipping to study the dress.

"My mother made them."

I went still.

Rhys smiled sadly at the shimmering gown. "She was a seamstress, back at the camp where she'd been raised. She didn't just do the work because she was ordered to. She did it because she loved it. And when she mated my father, she continued."

I grazed a reverent hand down my sleeve. "I—I had no idea."

His eyes were star-bright. "Long ago, when I was still a boy, she made them—all your gowns. A trousseau for my future bride." His throat bobbed. "Every piece . . . Every piece I have ever given you to wear, she made them. For you."

My eyes stung as I breathed, "Why didn't you tell me?"

He shrugged with one shoulder. "I thought you might be . . . disturbed to wear gowns made by a female who died centuries ago."

I put a hand over my heart. "I am honored, Rhys. Beyond words."

His mouth trembled a bit. "She would have loved you."

It was as great a gift as any I'd been given. I leaned down until our brows touched. *I would have loved her.*

I felt his gratitude without him saying a word as we remained there, breathing each other in for long minutes.

When I could finally speak again, I pulled away. "I've been thinking."

"Should I be worried?"

I slapped his boots, and he laughed, deep and rasping, the sound curling around my core.

I showed him my palms, the eye in both of them. "I want these changed."

"Oh?"

"Since you're no longer using them to snoop on me, I figured they could be something else."

He set a hand on his broad chest. "I never snoop."

"You're the greatest busybody I've ever met."

Another laugh. "And what, exactly, do you want on your palms?"

I smiled at the paintings I'd done on the walls, the mantel, the tables. Thought of the tapestry I'd bought. "I want a mountain—with three stars." The Night Court insignia. "The same that you have on your knees."

Rhys was quiet for a long time, his face unreadable. When he spoke, his voice was low. "Those are markings that can never be altered."

"It's a good thing I plan to be here for a while, then."

Rhys slowly sat up, unbuttoning the top of his tight black jacket. "You're sure?"

I nodded slowly.

He moved to stand before me, gently taking my hands in his, turning them palm-up. To the cat's eye that stared at us. "I never snooped, you know."

"You certainly did."

"Fine, I did. Can you forgive me?"

He meant it—the worry that I'd deemed his glimpses a violation. I rose onto my toes and kissed him softly. "I suppose I could find it in me."

"Hmmm." He brushed a thumb over the eye inked into both of my palms. "Any last words before I mark you forever?"

My heart thundered, but I said, "I have one last Solstice gift for you."

Rhys went still at my soft voice, the tremble in it. "Oh?"

Our hands linked, I caressed the adamant walls of his mind. The barriers immediately fell, allowing me in. Allowing me to show him that last gift.

What I hoped he'd deem as a gift, too.

His hands began shaking around mine, but he said nothing until I'd retreated from his mind. Until we were staring at each other again in silence.

His breathing turned ragged, his eyes silver-lined. "You're sure?" he repeated.

Yes. More than anything. I'd realized it, felt it, in the weaver's gallery. "Would it be . . . Would it indeed be a gift for you?" I dared ask.

His fingers tightened around mine. "Beyond measure."

As if in answer, light flared and sizzled along my palms, and I peered down to find my hands altered. The mountain and three stars gracing the heart of each palm.

Rhys was still staring at me, his breathing uneven.

"We can wait," he said quietly, as if fearful of the snow falling outside hearing our whispered words.

"I don't want to," I said, and meant it. The weaver had made me realize that, too. Or perhaps just see clearly what I'd quietly wanted for some time now.

"It could take years," he murmured.

"I can be patient." He lifted a brow at that, and I smiled, amending, "I can *try* to be patient."

His own answering smile set me grinning.

Rhys leaned in, brushing a kiss to my neck, right beneath my ear. "Shall we begin tonight, mate?"

My toes curled. "That was the plan."

"Mmm. Do you know what my plan was?" Another kiss, this one to the hollow of my throat as his hands slipped around my back and began to undo the hidden buttons of my dress. That precious, beautiful dress. I arched my neck to give him better access, and he obliged, his tongue flicking over the spot he'd just kissed.

"My plan," he went on, the dress sliding from me to pool on the rug, "involved this cabin, and a wall."

My eyes opened just as his hands began to trace long lines along my bare back. Lower.

I found Rhys smiling down at me, his eyes heavy-lidded while he surveyed my naked body. Naked, save for the diamond cuffs at my wrists. I went to remove them, but he murmured, "Leave them."

My stomach tightened in anticipation, my breasts turning achingly heavy.

I unbuttoned the rest of his jacket, fingers shaking, and peeled it from him, along with his shirt. And his pants.

Then he was standing naked before me, wings slightly flared, muscled chest heaving, showing me the full evidence of just how ready he was.

"Do you want to begin at the wall, or finish there?" His words were guttural, barely recognizable, and the gleam in his eyes turned into something predatory. He slid a hand down the front of my torso in brazen possessiveness. "Or shall it be the wall the entire time?"

My knees buckled, and I found myself beyond words. Beyond anything but him.

Rhys didn't wait for my answer before kneeling before me, his wings draping over the rug. Before he pressed a kiss to my abdomen, as if in reverence and benediction. Then pressed a kiss lower.

Lower.

My hand slid into his hair, just as he gripped one of my thighs and hoisted my leg over his shoulder. Just as I found myself somehow leaning against the wall near the doorway, as if he'd winnowed us. My head hit the wood with a soft thud as Rhys lowered his mouth to me.

He took his time.

Licked and stroked me until I'd shattered, then laughed against me, dark and rich, before he rose to his full height.

Before he hoisted me up, my legs wrapping around his waist, and pinned me against that wall.

One arm braced on the wall, the other holding me aloft, Rhys met my eyes. "How shall it be, mate?"

In his stare, I could have sworn galaxies swirled. In the shadows between his wings, the glorious depths of the night dwelled.

"Hard enough to make the pictures fall off," I reminded him, breathless.

He laughed again, low and wicked. "Hold on tight, then."

Mother above and Cauldron save me.

My hands slid onto his shoulders, digging into the hard muscle. But he slowly, *so slowly*, pushed into me.

So I felt every inch of him, every place where we were joined. I tipped my head back again, a moan slipping out of me.

"Every time," he gritted out. "Every time, you feel *exquisite*."

I clenched my teeth, panting through my nose. He worked his way in, thrusting in small movements, letting me adjust to each thick inch of him.

And when he was seated inside me, when his hand tightened on my hip, he just . . . stopped.

I moved my hips, desperate for any friction. He shifted with me, denying it.

Rhys licked his way up my throat. "I think about you, about this, every damn hour," he purred against my skin. "About the way you taste."

Another slight withdrawal—then a plunge in. I panted and panted, leaning my head into the hard wall behind me.

Rhys let out an approving sound, and withdrew slightly. Then pushed back in. Hard.

A low rattle sounded down the wall to my left.

I stopped caring. Stopped caring if we did indeed make the pictures fall off the wall as Rhys halted once more.

"But mostly I think about this. How you feel around me, Feyre." He drove into me, exquisite and relentless. "How you taste on my tongue." My nails cut into his broad shoulders. "How even if we have a thousand years together, I will never tire of *this*."

Release began to gather along my spine, shutting out all sound and sense beyond where he met me, touched me.

Another thrust, longer and harder. The wood groaned beneath his hand.

He lowered his mouth to my breast and nipped—nipped, and then licked away the hurt that sent pleasure zinging through my blood. "How you let me do such naughty, terrible things to you."

His voice was a caress that had my hips moving, begging him to go *faster*.

Rhys only chuckled softly, cruelly, as he withheld that all-out, unhinged joining I craved.

I opened my eyes long enough to peer down, to where I could see him joined with me, moving so achingly slowly in and out of me. "Do you like watching?" he breathed. "Watching me move in you?"

In answer, beyond words, I shot my mind down the bridge between us, brushing against his adamant shields.

He let me in instantly, mind-to-mind and soul-to-soul, and then I was looking through his eyes—looking down at *me* as he gripped my hip and thrust.

He purred, *Look at how I fuck you, Feyre.*

Gods, was my only answer.

Mental hands ran along my mind, my soul. *Look at how perfectly we fit.*

My flushed body was arched against the wall—perfect indeed for receiving him, for taking every inch of him.

Do you see why I can't stop thinking of this—of you?

Again, he withdrew and drove in, and released the damper on his power.

Stars flickered around us, sweet darkness sweeping in. As if we were the only souls in a galaxy. And still Rhys remained before me, my legs wrapped around his waist.

I brushed my own mental hands down him and breathed, *Can you fuck me in here, too?*

That wicked delight faltered. Went silent.

The stars and darkness paused, too.

Then undiluted, utter predator answered, *It would be my pleasure.*

And then I didn't have the words for what happened.

He gave me everything I wanted: the unleashed pounding of him inside my body—the unrelenting thrust and filling and slap of skin on skin, the slam of our bodies against wood. Night singing all around us, stars sweeping by like snow.

And then there was us. Mind-to-mind, lain out on that bridge between our souls.

We had no bodies here, but I felt him as he seduced me, his dark power wrapping around mine, licking at my flames, sucking on my ice, scraping claws against my own.

I felt him as his power blended with mine, ebbing and flowing, in and out, until my magic lashed out, latching onto him, both of us raging and burning together.

All while he moved in me, relentless and driving as the sea. Over and over, power and flesh and soul, until I think I was screaming, until I think he was roaring, and my mortal body clenched around him, shattering.

Then *I* shattered, everything I was rupturing into stars and galaxies and comets, nothing but pure, shining joy. Rhys held me, enveloped me, his darkness absorbing the light that sparkled and blasted, keeping me whole, keeping me together.

And when my mind could form words, when I could again feel his essence around me, his body still moving in my own, I sent him that image one last time, into the dark and stars—my gift.

Perhaps our gift, one day.

Rhys spilled into me with a roar, his wings splaying wide.

And in our minds, down that bond, his magic erupted, his soul washing over mine, filling every crack and pit so that there was not one part of me that was not full of him, brimming with his dark, glorious essence and undimming love.

He remained buried in me, leaning heavily against the wall as he panted against my neck, *"FeyreFeyreFeyre."*

He was shaking. We both were.

I worked up the presence of mind to crack open my eyes.

His face was wrecked. Stunned. His mouth remained partially open as he gaped at me, the glow still radiating from my skin, bright against the star-kissed shadows along his.

For long moments, we only stared. Breathed.

And then Rhys glanced sidelong toward the rest of the room.

Toward what we'd done.

A sly smile formed on his lips as we took in the pictures that had indeed come off the wall, their frames cracked on the floor. A vase atop a nearby side table had even been knocked to the ground, shattered into little blue pieces.

Rhys kissed beneath my ear. "That'll come out of your salary, you know."

I whipped my head to him and released my grip on his shoulders to flick his nose. He laughed, brushing his lips against my temple.

But I stared at the marks I'd left on his skin, already fading. Stared at the tattoos across his chest, his arms. Even an immortal's lifetime of painting wouldn't be enough to capture every facet of him. Of us.

I lifted my eyes to his again and found stars and darkness waiting. Found *home* waiting.

Never enough. Not to paint him, know him. Eons would never be enough for all I wanted to do, see with him. For all I wanted to love him.

The painting shone before me: *Night Triumphant—and the Stars Eternal.*

"Do it again," I breathed, my voice hoarse.

Rhys knew what I meant.

And I'd never been so glad for a Fae mate when he hardened again a heartbeat later, lowered me to the floor and flipped me onto my stomach, then plunged deep into me with a growling purr.

And even when we eventually collapsed on the rug, barely avoiding the broken pictures and vase shards, unable to move for a good long while, that image of my gift remained between us, shimmering as bright as any star.

That beautiful, blue-eyed, dark-haired boy that the Bone Carver had once shown me.

That promise of the future.

✢

Velaris was still sleeping when Rhys and I returned the next morning.

He didn't bring us to the town house, however. But to an estate along the river, the building in ruins, the gardens a tangle.

Mist hung over much of the city in the hour before dawn.

The words we'd exchanged last night, what we'd done, flowed between us, as invisible and solid as our mating bond. He hadn't taken his contraceptive tonic with breakfast. Wouldn't be taking it again anytime soon.

"You never asked about your Solstice present," Rhys said after a while, our steps crunching in the frosted gravel of the gardens along the Sidra.

I lifted my head from where I'd been leaning it against his shoulder while we'd ambled along. "I suppose you were waiting to make a dramatic reveal."

"I suppose I was." He halted, and I paused beside him as he turned to the house behind us. "This."

I blinked at him. At the rubble of the estate. "This?"

"Consider it a Solstice and birthday present in one." He gestured to the house, the gardens, the grounds that flowed to the river's edge. With a perfect view of the Rainbow at night, thanks to the land's curve. "It's yours. Ours. I purchased it on Solstice Eve. Workers are coming in two days to begin clearing the rubble and knock down the rest of the house."

I blinked again, long and slow. "You bought me an *estate*."

"Technically, it will be *our* estate, but the house is yours. Build it to your heart's content. Everything you want, everything you need—build it."

The cost alone, the sheer size of this gift had to be beyond astronomical. "Rhys."

He paced a few steps, running his hands through his blue-black hair, his wings tucked in tight. "We have no space at the town house. You and I can barely fit everything in the bedroom. And no one wants to be at the House of Wind." He again gestured to the magnificent estate around us. "So build a house for us, Feyre. Dream as wildly as you want. It's yours."

I didn't have words for it. What cascaded through me. "It—the *cost*—"

"Don't worry about the cost."

"But . . ." I gaped at the sleeping, tangled land, the ruined house. Pictured what I might want there. My knees wobbled. "Rhys—it's too much."

His face became deadly serious. "Not for you. Never for you." He slid his arms around my waist, kissing my temple. "Build a house with a painting studio." He kissed my other temple. "Build a house with an office for you, and one for me. Build a house with a bathtub big enough for two—and for wings." Another kiss, this time to my cheek. "Build a house with rooms for all our family." He kissed my other cheek. "Build a house with a garden for Elain, a training ring for the Illyrian babies, a library for Amren, and an enormous dressing room for Mor." I choked on a laugh at that. But Rhys silenced it with a kiss to my mouth, lingering and sweet. "Build a house with a nursery, Feyre."

My heart tightened to the point of pain, and I kissed him back. Kissed him again, and again, the property wide and clear around us. "I will," I promised.

CHAPTER
23

Rhysand

The sex had destroyed me.

Utterly ruined me.

Any lingering scrap of my soul that hadn't already belonged to her had unconditionally surrendered last night.

And seeing Feyre's expression when I showed her the riverfront estate . . . I held the memory of her shining, beautiful face close to me as I knocked on the cracked front doors of Tamlin's manor.

No answer.

I waited a minute. Two.

I unspooled a thread of power through the house, sensing. Half dreading what I might find.

But there—in the kitchens. A level below. Alive.

I saw myself in, my steps echoing on the splintered marble floors. I didn't bother to veil them. He likely sensed my arrival the moment I'd winnowed onto his front step.

It was a matter of a few minutes to reach the kitchen.

I wasn't entirely prepared for what I saw.

A great elk lay dead on the long worktable in the center of the dark space, the arrow through its throat illumined by the watery light leaking through the small windows. Blood pooled on the gray stone floor, its drip the only sound.

The only sound as Tamlin sat in a chair before it. Staring at the felled beast.

"Your dinner is leaking," I told him by way of greeting, nodding toward the mess gathering on the floor.

No reply. The High Lord of Spring didn't so much as look up at me.

Your mate should have known better than to kick a downed male.

Lucien's words to Feyre yesterday had lingered. Perhaps it was why I'd left Feyre to explore the new paints Azriel had given her and winnowed here.

I surveyed the mighty elk, its dark eyes open and glazed. A hunting knife lay embedded in the wood beside its shaggy head.

Still no words, not even a whisper of movement. Very well, then.

"I spoke to Varian, Prince of Adriata," I said, lingering on the other side of the table, the rack of antlers like a briar of thorns between us. "I requested that he ask Tarquin to dispatch soldiers to your border." I'd done it last night, pulling Varian aside during dinner. He'd readily agreed, swearing it would be done. "They will arrive within a few days."

No reply.

"Is that acceptable to you?" As part of the Seasonal Courts, Summer and Spring had long been allies—until this war.

Slowly, Tamlin's head lifted, his unbound golden hair dull and matted.

"Do you think she will forgive me?" The question was a rasp. As if he'd been screaming.

I knew whom he meant. And I didn't know. I didn't know if her

211

wishing him happiness was the same as forgiveness. If Feyre would ever want to offer that to him. Forgiveness could be a gift to both, but what he'd done . . . "Do you want her to?"

His green eyes were empty. "Do I deserve it?"

No. Never.

He must have read it on my face, because he asked, "Do you forgive me—for your mother and sister?"

"I don't recall ever hearing an apology."

As if an apology would ever right it. As if an apology would ever cover the loss that still ate at me, the hole that remained where their bright, lovely lives had once glowed.

"I don't think one will make a difference, anyway," Tamlin said, staring at the felled elk once more. "For either of you."

Broken. Utterly broken.

You will need Tamlin as an ally before the dust has settled, Lucien had warned my mate. Perhaps that was why I'd come, too.

I waved a hand, my magic slicing and sundering, and the elk's coat slid to the floor in a rasp of fur and slap of wet flesh. Another flicker of power, and slabs of meat had been carved from its sides, piled next to the dark stove—which soon kindled.

"Eat, Tamlin," I said. He didn't so much as blink.

It was not forgiveness—it was not kindness. I could not, would not, ever forget what he'd done to those I loved most.

But it was Solstice, or had been. And perhaps because Feyre had given me a gift greater than any I could dream of, I said, "You can waste away and die after we've sorted out this new world of ours."

A pulse of my power, and an iron skillet slid onto the now-hot stove, a steak of meat thumping into it with a sizzle.

"Eat, Tamlin," I repeated, and vanished on a dark wind.

CHAPTER
24

Morrigan

She'd lied to Feyre.

Sort of.

She *was* going to the Winter Court. Just not as soon as she'd said. Viviane, at least, knew when to truly expect her. Although they'd been exchanging letters for months now, Mor still hadn't told even the Lady of the Winter Court where she'd be between Solstice in Velaris and her visit to Viviane and Kallias's mountain home.

She didn't like telling people about this place. Had never mentioned it to the others.

And as Mor galloped over the snowy hills, her mare, Ellia, a solid, warm weight beneath her, she remembered why.

Early-morning mist hung between the bumps and hollows of the sprawling estate. Her estate. Athelwood.

She'd bought it three hundred years ago for the quiet. Had kept it for the horses.

Ellia took the hills with unfaltering grace, flowing fast as the west wind.

Mor hadn't been raised to ride. Not when winnowing was infinitely faster.

But with winnowing, it never felt as if she were actually *traveling* anywhere. As if she were going, running, racing to the next place. She wished it, and there she was.

The horses, though . . . Mor felt every inch of land they galloped across. Felt the wind and smelled the hills and snow and could see the passing wall of dense forest to her left.

Alive. It was all alive, and her ever more so, when she rode.

Athelwood had come with six horses, the previous owner having grown bored with them. All of them rare and coveted breeds. They'd been worth as much as the sprawling estate and three hundred pristine acres northwest of Velaris. A land of rolling hills and burbling streams, of ancient forests and crashing seas.

She did not like being alone for long periods of time—couldn't stand it. But a few days here and there were necessary, vital for her soul. And getting out on Ellia was as rejuvenating as any day spent basking in the sun.

She pulled Ellia to a halt atop one of the larger hills, letting the mare rest, even as Ellia yanked on the reins. She'd run until her heart gave out—had never been quite as docile as her handlers desired. Mor loved her all the greater for it.

She had always been drawn to the untamed, wild things of the world.

Horse and rider breathing hard, Mor surveyed her rolling grounds, the gray sky. Nestled in her Illyrian leathers and heated from the ride, she was comfortably warm. An afternoon reading by the crackling fire in Athelwood's extensive library followed by a hearty dinner and early bed would be bliss.

How far away the continent seemed, Rhys's request with it. To go, to play spy and courtier and ambassador, to see those kingdoms long closed, where friends had once dwelled . . . *Yes*, her blood called to her. *Go as far and wide as you can. Go on the wind.*

But to leave, to let Keir believe he had *made* her go with his bargain with Eris . . .

Coward. Pathetic coward.

She shut out the hissing in her head, running a hand down Ellia's snowy mane.

She had not mentioned it these past few days in Velaris. Had wanted to make this choice on her own, and had understood how the news might cast a shadow over the merriment.

She knew Azriel would say no, would want her safe. As he had always done. Cassian would have said yes, Amren with him, and Feyre would have worried but agreed. Az would have been pissed, and withdrawn even further into himself.

She hadn't wanted to take his joy away from him. Any more than she already did.

But she'd have to tell them, regardless of what she decided, at some point.

Ellia's ears went flat against her head.

Mor stiffened, following the mare's line of sight.

To the tangle of wood to their left, little more than a thatch of trees from this distance.

She rubbed Ellia's neck. "Easy," she breathed. "Easy."

Even in these woods, ancient terrors had been known to emerge.

But Mor scented nothing, saw nothing. The tendril of power she speared toward the woods revealed only the usual birds and small beasts. A hart drinking from a hole in an iced-over stream.

Nothing, except—

There, between a snarl of thorns. A patch of darkness.

It did not move, did not seem to do anything but linger. And watch.

Familiar and yet foreign.

Something in her power whispered not to touch it, not to go near it. Even from this distance.

Mor obeyed.

But she still watched that darkness in the thorns, as if a shadow had fallen asleep amongst them.

Not like Azriel's shadows, twining and whispering.

Something different.

Something that stared back, watching her in turn.

Best left undisturbed. Especially with the promise of a crackling fire and glass of wine at home.

"Let's take the short route back," she murmured to Ellia, patting her neck.

The horse needed no further encouragement before launching into a gallop, turning them from the woods and its shadowy watcher.

Over and between the hills they rode, until the woods were hidden in the mists behind them.

What else might she see, witness, in lands where none in the Night Court had ventured for millennia?

The question lingered with every thunderous step from Ellia over snow and brook and hill.

Its answer echoed off the rocks and trees and gray clouds overhead.

Go. Go.

CHAPTER
25

Feyre

Two days later, I stood in the doorway of Polina's abandoned studio.

Gone were the boarded-up windows, the drooping cobwebs. Only open space remained, clean and wide.

I was still gaping when Ressina found me, halting on her path down the street, no doubt coming from her own studio. "Happy Solstice, my lady," she said, smiling brightly.

I didn't return the smile as I stared and stared at the open door. The space beyond.

Ressina laid a hand on my arm. "Is something wrong?"

My fingers curled at my sides, wrapping around the brass key in my palm. "It's mine," I said quietly.

Ressina's smile began to grow again. "Is it, now?"

"They—her family gave it to me."

It had happened this morning. I'd winnowed to Polina's family farm, somehow surprising no one when I'd appeared. As if they'd been waiting.

Ressina angled her head. "So why the face?"

"They *gave* it to me." I splayed my arms. "I tried to buy it. I offered her family money." I shook my head, still reeling. I hadn't even been back to the town house. Hadn't even told Rhys. I'd woken at dawn, Rhys already off to meet with Az and Cassian at Devlon's camp, and decided to hell with waiting. Putting *life* off didn't make a lick of sense. I knew what I wanted. There was no reason to delay. "They handed me the deed, told me to sign my name to it, and gave me the key." I rubbed my face. "They refused my money."

Ressina let out a long whistle. "I'm not surprised."

"Polina's sister, though," I said, my voice shaking as I pocketed the key in my overcoat, "suggested I use the money for something else. That if I wanted to give it away, I should donate it to the Brush and Chisel. Do you know what that is?"

I'd been too stunned to ask, to do anything other than nod and say I would.

Ressina's ochre eyes softened. "It's a charity for artists in need of financial help—to provide them and their families with money for food or rent or clothes. So they needn't go hungry or want for anything while they create."

I couldn't stop the tears that blurred my vision. Couldn't stop myself from remembering those years in that cottage, the hollow ache of hunger. The image of those three little containers of paint that I'd savored.

"I didn't know it existed," I managed to whisper. Even with all the committees that I volunteered to help, they had not mentioned it.

I didn't know that there was a place, a world, where artists might be valued. Taken care of. I'd never dreamed of such a thing.

A warm, slender hand landed on my shoulder, gently squeezing.

Ressina asked, "So what are you going to do with it? The studio."

I surveyed the empty space before me. Not empty—*waiting*.

And from far away, as if it was carried on the cold wind, I heard the Suriel's voice.

Feyre Archeron, a request. Leave this world a better place than how you found it.

I swallowed down my tears, and brushed a stray strand of my hair back into my braid before I turned to the faerie. "You wouldn't be looking for a wholly inexperienced business partner, would you?"

Chapter
26

Rhysand

The girls were in the training ring.

Only six of them, and none looking too pleased, but they were there, cringing their way through Devlon's halfhearted orders on how to handle a dagger. At least Devlon had given them something relatively simple to learn. Unlike the Illyrian bows, a stack of them lingering by the girls' chalk-lined ring. As if in a taunt.

A good number of males couldn't muster the strength to wield those mighty bows. I could still feel the whip of the string against my cheek, my wrist, my fingers during the years it had taken to master it.

If one of the girls decided to take up the Illyrian bow, I'd oversee her lessons myself.

I lingered with Cassian and Azriel at the far end of the sparring rings, the Windhaven camp glaringly bright with the fresh snow that had been dumped by the storm.

As expected, the storm had finished yesterday—two days after Solstice. And as promised, Devlon had the girls in the ring. The youngest was around twelve, the eldest sixteen.

"I thought there were more," Azriel muttered.

"Some left with their families for Solstice," Cassian said, eyes on the training, hissing every now and then when one of the girls did a painfully wrong maneuver that went uncorrected. "They won't be back for a few more days."

We'd shown him the lists Az had compiled of the possible troublemakers in these camps. Cassian had been distant ever since. More malcontents than we'd expected. A good number of them from the Ironcrest camp, notorious rival of this clan, where Kallon, son of its lord, was taking pains to stir up as much dissent as possible. All directed toward Cassian and myself.

A ballsy move, considering Kallon was still a warrior-novice. Not even due to take the Rite until this spring or the next. But he was as bad as his brute of a father. Worse, Az claimed.

Accidents happen in the Rite, I'd only suggested when Cass's face had tightened with the news.

We won't dishonor the Rite by tampering with it, was his only reply.

Accidents happen in the skies all the time, then, Azriel had coolly countered.

If the whelp wants to bust my balls, he can grow a pair himself and do it to my face, Cassian had growled, and that was that.

I knew him well enough to leave him to it—to decide how and when to deal with Kallon.

"Despite the grumblings in the camps," I said to Cassian, gesturing toward the training rings. The males kept a healthy distance from where the few females trained, as if frightened of catching some deadly disease. Pathetic. "This *is* a good sign, Cass."

Azriel nodded his agreement, his shadows twining around him. Most of the camp women had ducked into their homes when he'd appeared.

A rare visit from the shadowsinger. Both myth and terror. Az looked just as displeased to be here, but he'd come when I asked.

It was healthy, perhaps, for Az to sometimes remember where he'd come from. He still wore the Illyrian leathers. Had not tried to get the tattoos removed. Some part of him was Illyrian still. Always would be. Even if he wished to forget it.

Cassian said nothing for a minute, his face a mask of stone. He'd been distant even before we'd gathered around the table in my mother's old house to deliver the report this morning. Distant since Solstice. I'd bet decent money on why.

"It will be a good sign," Cassian said at last, "when there are twenty girls out there and they've shown up for a month straight."

Az snorted softly. "I'll bet you—"

"No bets," Cassian said. "Not on this."

Az held Cassian's stare for a moment, cobalt Siphons flickering, and then nodded. Understood. This mission of Cassian's, hatched years ago and perhaps close to fruition . . . It went beyond bets for him. Went down to a wound that had never really healed.

I slung my arm around Cassian's shoulders. "Small steps, brother." I threw him a grin, knowing it didn't meet my eyes. "Small steps."

For all of us.

Our world might very well depend on it.

CHAPTER
27

Feyre

The city bells chimed eleven in the morning.

A month later, Ressina and I stood near the front door, both of us in nearly identical clothes: thick, long sweaters, warm leggings, and sturdy, shearling-lined work boots.

Boots that were already splattered with paint.

In the weeks since Polina's family had gifted me the studio, Ressina and I had been here nearly every day. Readying the place. Figuring out our strategy. The lessons.

"Any minute now," Ressina murmured, glancing to the small clock mounted on the bright white walls of the studio. *That* had been an endless debate: what color to paint the space? We'd wanted yellow, then decided that it might not display the art well enough. Black and gray were too dreary for the atmosphere we wanted, beige could also clash with the art . . . So we'd gone with white. The back room, at least, we'd painted brightly—a different color on each wall. Green and pink and red and blue.

But this front space . . . Empty. Save for the tapestry I'd hung on one wall, the black of the Void mesmerizing. And a reminder. As much of a reminder as the impossible iridescence of Hope, glittering throughout. To work through loss, no matter how overwhelming. To create.

And then there were the ten easels and stools set in a circle in the middle of the gallery floor.

Waiting.

"Will they come?" I murmured to Ressina.

The faerie shifted on her feet, the only sign of her worry. "They said they would."

In the month that we'd been working together, she'd become a good friend. A dear friend. Ressina's eye for design was impeccable, good enough that I'd asked her to help me plan the river-house. That's what I was calling it. Since *river-manor* . . . No. *House* it would be, even if it was the largest home in this city. Not from any preening, but simply from practicality. From the size of our court, our family. A family that would perhaps keep growing.

But that was later. For now . . .

A minute passed by. Then two.

"Come on," Ressina muttered.

"Perhaps they had the wrong time?"

But as I said it, they emerged. Ressina and I held our breath as the pack of them rounded the corner, aiming for the studio.

Ten children, High Fae and faerie, and some of their parents.

Some of them—since others were no longer alive.

I kept a warm smile on my face, even as my heart thundered with each child that passed through our door, wary and unsure, clustering near the easels. My palms sweated as the parents gathered with them, their faces less guarded, but still hesitant. Hesitant, yet hopeful.

Not just for themselves, but the children they'd brought with them.

We hadn't advertised broadly. Ressina had reached out to some friends and acquaintances, and requested they ask around. If there were children in this city who might need a place to express the horrors that had happened during the war. If there were children who might not be able to talk about what they'd endured, but could perhaps paint or draw or sculpt it. Perhaps they wouldn't do any of those things, but the act of creating *something* . . . it could be a balm to them.

As it was for me.

As it was for the weaver, and Ressina, and so many of the artists in this city.

Once word had gotten out, inquiries had poured in. Not just from parents or guardians, but from potential instructors. Artists in the Rainbow who were eager to help—to teach classes.

I'd instruct one a day, depending on what was required of me as High Lady. Ressina would do another. And a rotating schedule of other teachers to teach the third and fourth classes of the day. Including the weaver, Aranea, herself.

Because the response from parents and family had been overwhelming.

How soon do classes start? was the most frequent question. The close second being *How much does it cost?*

Nothing. Nothing, we told them. It was free. No child or family would ever pay for classes here—or the supplies.

The room filled, and Ressina and I swapped a quick, relieved look. A nervous look, too.

And when I faced the families gathered, the room open and sunny around us, I smiled once more and began.

CHAPTER
28

Feyre

He was waiting for me an hour and a half later.

As the last of the children flitted out, some laughing, some still solemn and hollow-eyed, he held the door open for them and their families. They all gawked, bowing their heads, and Rhys offered them a wide, easy smile in return.

I loved that smile. Loved that casual grace as he strode into the gallery, no sign of his wings today, and surveyed the still-drying paintings. Surveyed the paint splattered on my face and sweater and boots. "Rough day at the office?"

I pushed back a strand of my hair. Knowing it was likely streaked with blue paint. Since my fingers were covered in it. "You should see Ressina."

Indeed, she'd gone into the back moments ago to wash off a face full of red paint. Courtesy of one of the children, who'd deemed it a good idea to form a bubble of *all* the paint to see what color it would turn, and then float it across the room. Where it collided with her face.

Rhys laughed when I showed him down the bond. "Excellent use of their budding powers, at least."

I grinned, surveying one of the paintings beside him. "That's what I said. Ressina didn't find it so funny."

Though she had. Smiling had been a little difficult, though, when so many of the children had both visible and unseen scars.

Rhys and I studied a painting by a young faerie whose parents had been killed in the attack. "We didn't give them any detailed prompts," I said as Rhys's eyes roved around the painting. "We only told them to paint a memory. This is what she came up with."

It was hard to look at. The two figures in it. The red paint. The figures in the sky, their vicious teeth and reaching claws.

"They don't take their paintings home?"

"These will dry first, but I asked her if she wanted me to keep this somewhere special. She said to throw it out."

Rhys's eyes danced with worry.

I said quietly, "I want to keep it. To put in my future office. So we don't forget."

What had happened, what we were working for. Exactly why Aranea's tapestry of the Night Court insignia hung on the wall here.

He kissed my cheek in answer and moved to the next painting. He laughed. "Explain this one."

"This boy was *immensely* disappointed in his Solstice presents. Especially since it didn't include a puppy. So his 'memory' is one he hopes to make in the future—of him and his 'dog.' With his parents in a doghouse instead, while he and the dog live in the proper house."

"Mother help his parents."

"He was the one who made the bubble."

He laughed again. "Mother help *you*."

I nudged him, laughing now. "Walk me home for lunch?"

He sketched a bow. "It would be my honor, lady."

I rolled my eyes, shouting to Ressina that I'd be back in an hour. She called that I should take my time. The next class didn't come until two. We'd decided to both be at these initial classes, so the parents and guardians got to know us. And the children as well. It would be two full weeks of this before we got through the entire roster of classes.

Rhys helped me with my coat, stealing a kiss before we walked out into the sunny, frigid day. The Rainbow bustled around us, artists and shoppers nodding and waving our way as we strode for the town house.

I linked my arm through his, nestling into his warmth. "It's strange," I murmured.

Rhys angled his head. "What is?"

I smiled. At him, at the Rainbow, at the city. "This feeling, this excitement to wake up every day. To see you, and to work, and to just *be* here."

Nearly a year ago, I'd told him the opposite. Wished for the opposite. His face softened, as if he, too, remembered it. And understood.

I went on, "I know there's much to do. I know there are things we'll have to face. A few sooner than later." Some of the stars in his eyes banked at that. "I know there's the Illyrians, and the human queens, and the humans themselves, and all of it. But despite them . . ." I couldn't finish. Couldn't find the right words. Or speak them without falling apart in public.

So I leaned into him, into that unfailing strength, and said down the bond, *You make me so very happy. My* life *is happy, and I will never stop being grateful that you are in it.*

I looked up to find him not at all ashamed to have tears slipping down his cheeks in public. I brushed a few away before the chill wind could freeze them, and Rhys whispered in my ear, "I will never stop being grateful to have you in my life, either, Feyre darling. And no matter what lies ahead"—a small, joyous smile at that— "we will face it together. Enjoy every moment of it together."

I leaned into him again, his arm tightening around my shoulders. Around the top of the arm inked with the tattoo we both bore, the promise between us. To never part, not until the end.

And even after that.

I love you, I said down the bond.

What's not to love?

Before I could elbow him, Rhys kissed me again, breathless and swift. *To the stars who listen, Feyre.*

I brushed a hand over his cheek to wipe away the last of his tears, his skin warm and soft, and we turned down the street that would lead us home. Toward our future—and all that waited within it.

To the dreams that are answered, Rhys.

THE

A COURT
THORNS OF
ROSES AND

SERIES WILL CONTINUE.

READ ON FOR A SNEAK PEEK
OF THE NEXT BOOK.

The black water at her thrashing heels was freezing.

Not the bite of winter chill, or even the burn of solid ice, but something colder. Deeper.

It was the cold of the gaps between stars, the cold of a world before light.

The cold of hell—true hell, she realized, as she bucked and kicked against the strong hands trying to shove her into that Cauldron.

True hell, because that was Elain lying on the floor, the red-haired, one-eyed Fae male hovering over her. Because those were pointed ears poking through the sodden gold-brown hair, and that was an immortal glow resting upon Elain's fair skin.

True hell, worse than the inky depths that waited mere inches from her toes.

Put her in, the hard-faced king ordered.

And the sound of that voice, the male who had done this to Elain . . .

She knew that she was going into the Cauldron. Knew she would lose this fight.

Knew no one was coming to save her, not sobbing Feyre, not Feyre's gagged former lover, not her devastated new mate. Not Cassian, broken and bleeding on the floor, still trying to rise on trembling arms.

The king—he had done this. To Elain. To Cassian.

And to her.

The icy water bit into the soles of her feet.

It was a bite of venom, a bite of a death so permanent that every inch of her roared in defiance.

She was going in, but she would not go gently. She would not go bowed to this Fae king.

The water gripped her ankles with phantom hands, tugging her down.

So she twisted, wrenching her arm free from the guard who held it.

And so she pointed.

One finger—at the king.

Down down down that water wanted to pull her.

But Nesta Archeron still pointed at the King of Hybern.

A death-promise. A target marked.

Hands shoved her into the water's awaiting claws.

And Nesta Archeron laughed at the fear that crept into the king's eyes. Just before the water devoured her whole.

In the beginning
And at the end
There was Darkness
And nothing more

She did not feel the cold as she sank into a sea of blackness that had no bottom, no horizon, no surface.

But she felt the burning when it began.

Immortality was not a serene youth.

It was fire.

It was molten ore poured into her veins, boiling up her human blood until it was nothing but steam, forging her brittle bones into fresh steel.

When she opened her mouth to scream, when the pain ripped apart her very self, there was no sound. There was nothing here, in this place, but darkness and agony and power—

Not gently.

She would not take this gently.

She would not *let* them do this. To her, to Elain.

She would not bow, or yield, or grovel.

They would pay. All of them.

Starting with this *place*, this *thing*.

Starting *now*.

She tore into the darkness with claws and talons and teeth. Rent and cleaved and shredded.

The dark eternity around her shuddered. Bucked. Thrashed.

She laughed as it tried to recoil. Laughed around the mouthful of raw power she ripped from the inky black around her and swallowed whole; laughed at the fistfuls of eternity she shoved into her heart, her veins.

The Cauldron struggled like a bird under a cat's paw. She refused to relent her grip.

Everything it had stolen from her, from Elain, she would take from it. From Hybern.

So she did.

Down into black eternity, Nesta and the Cauldron twined and fell, burning through the darkness like a newborn star.

Cassian raised his fist to the green-painted door in the dim hallway—and hesitated.

He'd cut down more enemies than he could count or remember, had stood knee-deep in gore on a killing field and kept swinging, had made choices that cost him the lives of good warriors, had been a general and a grunt and an assassin, and yet here he was, lowering his fist. Balking.

The building on the north side of the Sidra was in need of new paint. And new floors, if the creaking boards beneath his boots had been any indication as he'd climbed the two flights. But at least it was clean. It was still grim by Velaris standards, but when the city itself had no slums, that wasn't saying much. He'd seen and stayed in far worse.

But it didn't quite explain *why* she was staying here. Had insisted she live here, when the town house was sitting empty thanks to the river estate's completion. He could understand why she wouldn't bother taking up rooms in the House of Wind—it was too far from the city, and she couldn't fly or winnow in. But Feyre and Rhys gave her a salary. The same, generous one they gave him, and every member of their circle. So Cassian knew she could afford far, far better.

He frowned at the peeling paint on the green door before him. No sounds trickled through the sizable gap between the door and floor; no fresh scents lingered in the hallway. Maybe he'd get lucky and she'd be out. Maybe she was still sleeping under the bar of whatever pleasure hall she'd frequented last night. Though maybe that'd be worse, since he'd have to track her down there, too. And a public scene . . .

He lifted his fist again, the red of his Siphon flickering in the ancient balls of faelight tucked into the ceiling.

Coward. Grow some damned balls and do your job.

Cassian knocked.

Once. Twice.

Silence.

Cassian almost sighed. Thank the Mother—

Clipped, precise footsteps thudded toward the other side of the door. Each more pissed off than the last.

He tucked his wings in tight, squaring his shoulders as he braced his feet slightly farther apart.

She had *four* locks on her door, and the snap as she unlatched each of them might as well have been the beating of a war-drum. He ran through the list of things he was to say, *how* Feyre had suggested he say them, but—

The door yanked open, the knob twisting so hard Cassian wondered if she was imagining it was his neck.

Nesta Archeron was already frowning.

But there she was. And she looked like hell.

"What do you want?" She didn't open the door wider than a hand's length.

When the hell had he last seen her? The end-of-summer party on that barge in the Sidra last month? She hadn't looked this bad. Though a night trying to drown oneself in alcohol never left anyone looking particularly good the next morning. Especially when it was—

"It's seven in the morning," she hissed, looking him over with that gray-blue stare that was usually kindling to his temper. "Come back later."

Indeed, she was in a male's shirt. That definitely didn't belong to her.

He braced a hand on the threshold and gave her a lazy grin he knew brought out the best in her. "Rough night?"

Rough year, he almost said. Because that beautiful face was indeed still pale, thinner than it'd been before the war, her lips bloodless, and those eyes . . . Cold and sharp, like a winter morning. No joy, no laughter, in any plane of her exquisite face.

"Come back in the afternoon," she said, making to slam the door on his hand.

Cassian shoved out a foot before she could break his fingers. Her nostrils flared slightly.

"Feyre wants you at the house."

"Which one," Nesta said flatly, frowning at the foot he'd wedged there. "She has three, after all."

He bit back the retort and the questions. This wasn't the selected battlefield, and he wasn't her opponent. No, his job was just to *get* her to the assigned spot. And then pray that the lovely riverfront home Feyre and Rhys had just moved into wouldn't be reduced to rubble.

"She's at the new one."

"Why didn't she come get me herself?" He knew that suspicious gleam in her eyes, the slight stiffening in her back. It had his own instincts surging to meet them, to push and push and see what might happen.

"Because she is High Lady of the Night Court, and she's busy running the territory."

Fine. Maybe they'd have a skirmish right here, right now.

A nice prelude to the battle ahead.

Nesta angled her head, golden-brown hair sliding over her too-thin shoulder. On anyone else, the movement would have been contemplative. On her, it was a predator sizing up prey.

"And my sister," she said in that flat voice that refused to yield any sign of emotion, "deemed that meeting her *right now* was necessary?"

"She knew you'd likely need to clean yourself up, and wanted you to get a head start. You're expected at eleven."

He waited for the explosion as she took in the words, did the math.

Her pupils flared. "Do I *look* like I need *four hours* to become presentable?"

He took the invitation to survey her: long, bare legs, an elegant sweep of hips, tapered waist—again, too damn thin—and full, inviting breasts that were so at odds with the sharp angles of her bones. On any other female, he might have called the combination mouthwatering. Might have begun courting her from the moment he'd met her.

But from the moment he'd met Nesta, the cold fire in her blue-gray eyes had been a temptation of a different sort. And now that she was High Fae, that inherent dominance, the aggression—and that piss-poor attitude . . . There was a reason he avoided her as much as possible. Even after the war, things were still too volatile, both within the Night Court's borders and in the world beyond. And the female before him had always made him feel like he was standing in quicksand.

Cassian said at last, "You look like you could use a few big meals, a bath, and some real clothes."

She rolled her eyes, but fingered the shirt she wore.

Cassian added, "Eleven o'clock. Kick the sorry prick out of here, get washed, and I'll bring you breakfast myself."

Her brows rose slightly.

He gave her a half-smile. "You think I can't hear that male in your bedroom, trying to quietly put on his clothes and sneak out the window?"

As if in answer, a muffled thud came from the bedroom. Nesta hissed.

Cassian said, "I'll be back in an hour to see how things are proceeding." He put enough bite behind the words that his soldiers would know not to push him, that he wore seven Siphons for a damned good reason. But Nesta did not fly in his legions, did not train under his command, and certainly did not seem to bother to remember that he was five hundred years old and—

"Don't bother. I'll be there on time."

He pushed off the door, wings flaring slightly as he retreated a few steps and grinned in that way he knew made her see red. "That's not what I was asked to do. I'm to see you from door to door."

Her face indeed tightened. "Go perch on a chimney."

He sketched a bow, not daring to take his eyes off her. She'd emerged from that Cauldron with gifts. Considerable, dark gifts. And though she had not used them, or explained to even Feyre and Amren what they were, or even shown a hint of them in the year since the war . . . he knew better than to make himself vulnerable to another predator. "Do you want your tea with milk or lemon?"

She slammed the door in his face.

Then locked each of those four locks. Slowly. Loudly.

Whistling to himself, wondering if that poor bastard inside the apartment would indeed flee out the window—mostly to escape *her*—Cassian strode down the dim hallway, and went to find some food.

He'd need it today, too—especially once Nesta learned precisely why her sister had summoned her.

+

Nesta Archeron didn't know the male's name.

She ransacked her wine-soaked memory as she strode for the bedroom, dodging columns of books and piles of clothing, recalling heated glances at the tavern, the initial wet, hot meeting of their mouths, the sweat coating her as she rode him until pleasure and drink sent her into oblivion, but . . . not the name.

The male was already at the window, Cassian no doubt lurking on the street below to witness this spectacularly pathetic exit, when Nesta reached the dim, cramped bedroom. The sheets on the brass poster bed were rumpled, half-spilled on the creaky wood floor, and the cracked window was already open as the male turned to her.

Handsome, in the way most Fae males were handsome. A bit thinner than she liked them—practically a boy compared to the towering mass of muscle that had just lurked outside her door. He winced as she padded in, and gave a pointed look to her shirt. "I . . . That's . . ."

Nesta reached over her head and tugged off his shirt, leaving nothing but bare skin in its wake. His eyes widened, but the scent of his fear remained—not at her, but at who he'd heard at the front door. As he remembered who *she* was, both in the court, and to Cassian. She chucked his white shirt to him. "You can use the front door now."

He swallowed, slinging the shirt over his head. "I—is he still—" His gaze kept snagging on her breasts, peaked against the chill morning, her bare skin. The apex of her thighs.

"Good-bye," was all Nesta said, striding for the rusty and leaky bathroom attached to her bedroom. At least the place had hot running water.

Sometimes.

Feyre and the others had tried to convince her to move more times than she could count. Each time, she'd ignored it.

Elain was happily ensconced in the new riverfront estate, and had spent the spring and summer planning and nurturing its spectacular gardens—all while avoiding her mate—but Nesta . . . She was immortal, she was beautiful, and she had no intention of beginning an eternity of working for these people anytime soon. Before she'd gotten to enjoy all that the Fae had to offer.

She had no doubt Feyre planned a scolding at their little *meeting* today.

After all, Nesta had signed the outrageous tab at the pleasure hall last night to her sister's account. But neither Feyre nor her mate would do anything about it beyond idle threats.

Nesta snorted, twisting the ancient faucet in the bath. It groaned, the metal icy to the touch, and water sputtered—then sprayed into the cracked, stained tub.

This was her place. No servants, no eyes monitoring and judging every move, no company unless . . . Unless busybody, puffed-up warriors made it their business to stop by.

It took five minutes for the water to actually heat enough to fill the tub. That she would even get into it was the biggest accomplishment she'd made in the past year. It had begun with willing herself, *forcing* herself to put in her feet. Then, each time, going a little further. Until she'd been able to stomach sitting fully submerged in the tub without her heart thundering. It had taken her months to get that far.

Today, at least, she slid into the hot water with little hesitation. By the time she'd finished washing away the sweat and other remnants of last night, a glance in the bedroom revealed the male had indeed taken the window out.

The sex hadn't been bad. She'd had better, but also had much worse. Immortality still wasn't enough to teach some males the art of the bedroom.

So she'd taught herself. Starting with the first male she'd taken here, who had no idea that her maidenhead was intact until he'd spied the speckled blood on the sheets. His face had gone white with terror—pure, ghastly white.

Not for fear of Feyre and Rhysand's wrath.

But the wrath of that insufferable Illyrian brute.

Everyone somehow knew what had happened during the war; that final battle with Hybern.

That Cassian had nearly bled out defending her against the

King of Hybern, that she'd chosen to shield him with her body in those last moments.

They had never spoken of it.

She still barely spoke to anyone about anything, let alone the war.

Yet as far as anyone was now concerned, the events of that last battle had bound them. Her and Cassian. No matter that she could scarcely stand to be around him. No matter that she had once, long ago, in a mortal body and in a house that no longer existed, let him kiss her throat. Being near him made her want to shatter things.

As her power sometimes did, unbidden. Secretly.

Nesta surveyed the ramshackle, dark apartment, the sagging and filthy furniture that had come with it, the clothes and dishes she left untended.

Rhysand had offered her jobs. Positions.

She didn't want them.

They were pity offerings, some attempt to get her to be a part of their life, to be gainfully occupied. Done not because Rhysand particularly liked her, but because he loved Feyre that much. No, the High Lord had never liked her—and their conversations were coldly civil at best.

So any offering, she knew, was made to appease his mate. Not because Nesta was truly needed for it. Truly . . . wanted.

Better to spend her time the way she wished to. They kept paying for it, after all.

The knock on the door rattled the entire apartment.

She glared toward the front room, debating pretending she'd left, but . . . he could hear her, smell her.

And if Cassian broke down the door, which he was likely to do, she'd just have the headache of explaining it to her stingy landlord.

So she freed all four locks.

Locking them each night was part of the ritual. Even when the nameless male had been here, even with the wine, she'd remembered to lock them all. Some muscle memory buried deep. She'd installed them that first day she'd arrived months and months ago, and had locked them every night since.

Nesta yanked open the door enough to spy Cassian's cocky grin and left it ajar as she stormed back inside for her shoes.

He took the unspoken invitation and walked in, a mug of tea in his hand—the cup no doubt borrowed from the shop at the corner. Or outright given to him, considering how people tended to worship the ground his muddy boots walked on.

He surveyed the squalor and let out a low whistle. "You do know that you could hire a maid, don't you?"

She scanned the small living area for her shoes—a sagging couch, a soot-stained hearth, a moth-eaten armchair—then the cracked and ancient kitchenette, then traced her steps into her bedroom. Where had she kicked them last night?

"Some fresh air would be a good start," he added from the other room, the window groaning as he no doubt cracked it open to let in the early-autumn breeze.

She found her shoes in opposite corners of the bedroom. One reeked of spilled wine and ale.

Nesta perched on the edge of her bed, sliding on her shoes, tugging at the laces. She didn't bother to look up as Cassian's steady steps approached, then halted at the threshold.

He sniffed once. Loudly.

It said enough.

"I'd hoped you at least changed the sheets between visitors, but . . . apparently that doesn't bother you, either."

She tied the lace on the first shoe and looked up at him beneath lowered brows. "Again, what business is it of yours?"

He shrugged, though the tightness on his face didn't reflect it. "If I can smell a few different males in here, then surely your . . . companions can, too."

"Hasn't stopped them yet." She tied the other shoe, Cassian's hazel eyes tracking the movement.

"Your tea is getting cold," he said through his teeth.

She ignored him and rose to her feet, searching the bedroom again. Her coat . . .

"Your coat is on the floor by the front door," he said sharply. "And it's going to be brisk out, so bring a scarf."

She ignored that, too, but strode past him, careful to avoid touching him, and found her dark blue overcoat exactly where he'd said it was. Only a few days ago had summer begun to yield to fall, drastically enough that she'd needed to pull out her warmer attire.

Nesta yanked open the front door, pointing for him to go.

Cassian held her gaze as he strode for her, then reached out an arm—

And plucked the cerulean-and-cream scarf Elain had given her for her birthday this spring off the brass hook on the wall. He gripped it in his fist as he stalked out, the scarf dangling like a strangled snake.

Something was eating at him. Usually, Cassian held out a bit longer before yielding to his temper. Perhaps it had to do with whatever Feyre wanted to tell her up at the house.

Her gut twisted a bit as she strode into the hall and set each lock, including the magical one Feyre had insisted Rhys install, linked to her blood and will.

She wasn't stupid—she knew there had been unrest, both in

Prythian and on the continent, since the war had ended. Knew some Fae territories were pushing their new limits on what they could get away with in terms of territory claims and how they treated humans.

But if some new threat had arisen . . .

Nesta shoved out the thought. She'd think about it when the time came. *If* the time came. No use wasting her energy on a phantom fear.

The four locks seemed to laugh at her before she silently followed Cassian out of the building, and into the bustling city beyond.

⊹

The riverfront house was more of an estate, and so new and clean and beautiful that Nesta realized that she was wearing two-day-old clothes, hadn't washed her hair, and her shoes were indeed covered in stale wine precisely as she strode through the towering marble archway and into the shining white-and-sand-colored front hall.

A sweeping staircase bisected the enormous space, either side of it shaped like a pair of spread wings, and a chandelier of hand-blown Velaris glass fashioned after a cluster of shooting stars drooped from the carved ceiling to meet it. The faelights in each golden orb cast shimmering reflections on the polished white marble floors, interrupted only by potted plants, wood furniture *also* made in Velaris, and art-art-art. Plush blue rugs broke up the perfect floors, a long runner leading down the cavernous hallway on either side of the entry, and one flowing straight beneath the stairs—to the sloping lawn and gleaming river beyond.

Trailing Cassian, Nesta headed to the left—toward the formal rooms for *business*, Feyre had told her, during that first and only tour two months ago.

She'd been half-drunk at the time, and had hated every second of it, every perfect, happy room.

Most males bought their wives and mates jewelry for an outrageous Solstice present.

Rhys had bought Feyre a palace.

No—he'd purchased the war-decimated property, and then given his mate free rein to design the residence of *both* their dreams.

And somehow, Nesta thought as she silently followed an unnaturally quiet Cassian down the hall toward one of the studies whose doors were already open, Feyre and Rhys *had* managed to make this place seem cozy, welcoming. A behemoth of a building, but a *home*, somehow.

Even the formal furniture, while beautiful, seemed designed for comfort and lounging, for long conversations over good food. Every piece of art had been picked by Feyre herself, or painted by her, so many of them portraits and depictions of *them*—her friends, her new family.

There was not one of her, naturally.

Even their gods-damned father had a picture in here, with him and Elain, smiling and happy, as they'd been before the world went to shit.

But during that tour, Nesta had noted the lack of herself here. Said nothing, of course, but it was a pointed absence.

It was enough to set her teeth on edge as Cassian slipped inside the study and said to whoever was inside, "She's here."

Nesta braced herself for whatever waited within, but Feyre merely chuckled and said, "You're five minutes early. I'm impressed."

"Seems like a good omen for gambling. We should head to Rita's," Cassian drawled just as Nesta stepped into the wood-paneled room.

The study opened into a garden courtyard, the space warm and merry and rich, and Nesta might have admitted that she liked the floor-to-ceiling oak bookshelves, the plush green-velvet furniture before the pale marble hearth, had she not seen who was sitting inside.

Feyre perched on the couch, clad in a heavy cream sweater and dark leggings.

Rhys, clad in his usual black, leaned against the marble mantel, arms crossed.

And Amren, in her usual gray—cross-legged in the Illyrian armchair by the roaring hearth, those uptilted silver eyes sweeping over Nesta with distaste. So much had changed between her and the small lady, perhaps more than any other relationship.

Nesta didn't let herself think about that argument at the end-of-summer party on the river barge. Or the silence between her and Amren since then.

Feyre, at least, smiled. "I heard you had quite the night."

Nesta merely glanced between where Cassian took a seat in the armchair across from Amren, the empty spot on the couch beside Feyre, and where Rhys stood by the hearth.

In far more formal clothes than he usually wore.

The High Lord's clothes.

Even if the High Lady of the Night Court was in attire fit for lounging on the sunny autumn day around them.

Nesta kept her spine straight, her chin high, hating that they all stared at her as she sat on the couch beside her sister. Hating that Rhys and Amren undoubtedly noted the filthy shoes, scented her old clothes, and probably still smelled that male on her.

"You look horrible," Amren said.

Nesta wasn't stupid enough to glare.

So she simply ignored her.

"Though it's hard to look good," Amren went on, "when you're out until the darkest hours of the night, drinking yourself stupid and fucking anything that comes your way."

Feyre whipped her head to the High Lord's Second. But Rhysand looked inclined to agree with Amren.

Cassian, at least, kept his mouth shut, and before Feyre could say anything to confirm or deny it, Nesta beat them to it and said, "I wasn't aware that my physical looks were under your jurisdiction."

Cassian loosed a breath that sounded like a warning.

Amren's silver eyes glowed, a small remnant of the terrible power she'd once wielded. "They are when you spend that many of our gold marks on wine and garbage."

Perhaps she had pushed them too far with last night's tab. Interesting.

Nesta looked to Feyre, who was wincing on the other end of the couch. "So you made me come to *you* for a scolding?"

Feyre's eyes—the eyes they both shared—seemed to soften slightly. "No. It's not a scolding." She cut a sharp glance at Rhys, still icily silent against the mantel, and then to Amren, seething in her chair. "Think of this as a . . . discussion."

"I don't see how my life is any of your concern, or up for any sort of *discussion*," Nesta bit out, and shot to her feet.

"*Sit down*," Rhys snarled.

And the raw command in that voice, the utter dominance and power . . .

Nesta froze, fighting it, hating that Fae part of her that bowed to such things. Cassian leaned forward in his chair, as if he'd leap between them.

But Nesta held Rhysand's lethal gaze. Threw every ounce of defiance she could into it, even as his order held her still. Made her knees *want* to bend, to sit.

Rhys said too quietly, "You are going to sit. You are going to listen."

She let out a low laugh. "You're not my High Lord. You don't give me orders."

But she knew how powerful he was. Had seen it, felt it. Still trembled to be near him. The most powerful High Lord in history.

Rhys scented that fear. She knew it from the second one side of his mouth curled up in a cruel smile.

"That's enough," Feyre said, more to Rhys than her. Then indeed snapped at her mate, "I told you to keep out of it."

He dragged those star-flecked eyes to Feyre, and it was all Nesta could do to keep from collapsing onto the couch as her knees gave out.

Feyre angled her head at her mate, nostrils flaring. "You can either *leave*," she hissed at him, "or you can stay and keep your mouth shut."

Rhys just crossed his arms. But said nothing.

"You too," Feyre spat in Amren's direction.

The little female harrumphed and nestled back in her chair.

Nesta didn't bother to look pleasant as Feyre twisted to face her. Her sister swallowed. "We need to make some changes, Nesta," Feyre said hoarsely. "You do—and *we* do."

They were kicking her out. Throwing her into the wild, perhaps to go back to the human lands—

"I'll take the blame," Feyre went on, "for things getting this far, and getting this bad. After the war, with everything else that was going on, it . . . you . . . *I* should have been there to help you, but I wasn't, and I am ready to admit that this is partially my fault."

"That *what* is your fault," Nesta demanded.

"You," Cassian said from the armchair to her left. "This bullshit behavior."

Her spine locked up, fire boiled in her veins at the insult, the *arrogance*—

"I understand how you're feeling," Feyre cut in.

"You know *nothing* about how I'm feeling," Nesta snapped.

"It's time for some changes." Feyre plowed ahead. "Starting *now*."

"Keep your self-righteous do-gooder nonsense out of my life."

"You don't have a life," Feyre retorted. "You have quite the opposite. And I'm not going to sit by and watch you destroy yourself for another moment."

"Oh?"

Rhys tensed at the sneer, but said nothing, as he'd promised.

"I want you out of Velaris," Feyre breathed, her voice shaking.

Nesta tried—tried and failed—not to feel the blow, the sting of the words. Though she didn't know why she was surprised by it.

There were no paintings of her in this house, they did not invite her to parties or dinners anymore, they certainly didn't visit—

"And where," Nesta asked, her voice mercifully icy, "am I supposed to go?"

Feyre only looked to Cassian.

And for once, the Illyrian warrior wasn't grinning as he said, "You're coming with me to the Illyrian Mountains."

ACKNOWLEDGMENTS

In the course of writing this tale, I wound up going through two of the biggest events of my life. This past summer, I was about a third of the way into drafting *A Court of Frost and Starlight* when I got the worst sort of phone call from my mom: my father had suffered a massive heart attack, and it was unlikely that he would survive. What happened next was nothing short of a miracle, and the fact that my dad is alive today to see this book come out fills me with more joy than I can express.

The incredible ICU team at the University of Vermont in Burlington will forever have my deepest gratitude. Not only for saving my father's life, but also for the unparalleled care and compassion that he (and my entire family) received during the two weeks we spent camped out in the hospital. The ICU nurses will always be my heroes—your tireless hard work, unfailing positivity, and remarkable intelligence are the stuff of legends. You offered my family a ray of hope during the darkest days of our lives, and never once made us feel the tremendous weight of the odds stacked against us.

Thank you, thank you, thank you for all that you do and have done, both for my family and for countless others.

I managed to finish writing *A Court of Frost and Starlight* after that (thanks to a few healing weeks spent up in beautiful Maine), but it wasn't until early autumn that the second life-changing thing happened: I found out that I was pregnant. To go from a summer that ranks among the worst days of my life to that sort of joy was such an enormous blessing, and though this tale will release a few weeks before I'm due to give birth, *A Court of Frost and Starlight* will always hold a special place in my heart because of it.

But I couldn't have gotten through these long months of working on this project without my husband, Josh. (I couldn't get through *life* without Josh.) So, thank you to the greatest husband in any world, for taking such good care of me, both before and during this pregnancy, and making sure that I had everything I needed to stay focused and make this book a reality (some prime examples: endless plates of snacks, tea on demand, finding me the comfiest of pillows to prop my swollen feet on). I love you to the stars and back, and I can't wait for this next epic chapter in our journey together.

And Annie. My sweet, sassy babypup, Annie. Thank you for the warm cuddles and whiskery kisses, for being such a joy and a comfort on both the brightest and darkest of days. There is no greater or more faithful canine companion than you. I love you forever.

As always, I owe a huge debt to my agent, Tamar Rydzinski. Thank you, thank you, thank you for being in my corner, for keeping me sane, and for your wisdom and guidance. None of this would be possible without you.

To the badass team at the Laura Dail Literary Agency: you guys rock. Thank you for *everything*. And Cassie Homer: you are the absolute best, and I am so grateful for all that you do.

Bethany Buck: thank you for all your help with this book, and for being such a lovely person. And thank you x infinity to the entire team at Bloomsbury: Cindy Loh, Cristina Gilbert, Kathleen Farrar, Nigel Newton, Rebecca McNally, Sonia Palmisano, Emma Hopkin, Ian Lamb, Emma Bradshaw, Lizzy Mason, Courtney Griffin, Erica Barmash, Emily Ritter, Alona Fryman, Alexis Castellanos, Grace Whooley, Alice Grigg, Elise Burns, Jenny Collins, Beth Eller, Kelly de Groot, Lucy Mackay-Sim, Hali Baumstein, Melissa Kavonic, Diane Aronson, Donna Mark, John Candell, Nicholas Church, Anna Bernard, Kate Sederstrom, and the entire foreign rights team: I'm so thrilled to be published by you.

Charlie Bowater: Your art is such an inspiration to me on so many levels. Thank you for all of your tremendous work, and for the truly stunning border on the cover. It's such a dream come true to collaborate with you, and I can't wait to work with you more in the future.

To my family: Thank you for the love and support you gave my dad and me this summer. You flew and drove in from all across the country to be there for us in Vermont, and almost a year later, I still don't have the words to convey my gratitude or how much I love you all. I am so very blessed to have you in my life.

To my parents: it's been one hell of a year, but we made it. I'll never stop being amazed and grateful that I can even say those words. I love you both.

To my marvelous friends (you know who you are): Thank you for being there when I needed you most, for checking on me and my family, and for never failing to bring a smile to my face.

And lastly, to everyone out there who has picked up my books: thank you. You are the greatest group of people that I've ever met, and I'm honored to have you as readers. To the stars who listen—and the dreams that are answered.

EXCITED FOR THE NEXT
A COURT OF THORNS AND ROSES
INSTALLMENT?

CHECK OUT THE

THRONE
OF
GLASS

SERIES WHILE YOU WAIT!

QUEEN OF SHADOWS

**The Goodreads Choice Award Winner for Best
Young Adult Fantasy and Science Fiction for 2015**

"Character motivations and interactions . . . are always nuanced and on point, especially as Aelin's growing maturity offers her new perspectives on old acquaintances. . . . Impossible to put down." —*Kirkus Reviews*

"Fans of the high-fantasy series likely won't mind the protracted story at all, packed as it is with brooding glances, simmering sexual tension, twisty plot turns, lush world building, and snarky banter." —*Booklist*

EMPIRE OF STORMS

**An Amazon Best Book
A BuzzFeed Best Book**

"Tightly plotted, delightful escapism." —*Kirkus Reviews*

"Fans devoted to the series (and there are many) will be eager for this installment's cinematic action, twisty schemes, and intense revelations of secrets and legacies." —*Booklist*

"More adventure and romance await fans of Maas's high-fantasy series in this . . . fifth installment of Aelin's epic journey to save humanity." —*The Horn Book Guide*

TOWER OF DAWN

**An Amazon Best Book
A Barnes & Noble Best Book**

"Turns a corner from sprawling epic to thrilling psychological fantasy." —*HuffPost*

"Will leave readers spellbound." —*RT Book Reviews*

www.bloomsbury.com
Twitter: BloomsburyKids
Snapchat: BloomsburyYA